AND STRANGE AT ECBATAN THE TREES

ALSO BY Michael Bishop

A Funeral for the Eyes of Fire

To Jeri

And strange at Ecbatan the trees
Take leaf by leaf the evening strange
Archibald MacLeish

AND STRANGE AT ECBATAN THE TREES

i

I went with the old man because Our Shathra Anna's foremost minister had bade me watch his every move. For ten days I had been at the old man's side, and uncomplainingly, though not very congenially (though this was changing), he had accepted my presence. The old man's name was Gabriel Elk. He was sixty-three years old. He was universally acknowledged a genius, perhaps the only bonafide one in all of Ongladred, indeed on all of our ruthlessly harsh planet, Mansueceria.

And on the night with which this account begins Gabriel Elk and I were going into Lunn, our capital, to buy a dead masker.

The city lay before us as ominously quiescent as an unstruck gong. I had been living—these past ten days—with

Gabriel Elk, his wife, Bethel, and his son, Gareth, at Stone-lore, the neuro-theatre he had built nearly seven kilometers outside of Lunn. Now we were coming back into the city under the cold light of the Shattered Moons, and I was glad to see Lunn's majestic squalor again, the unbroken rows of four-story dwellings, the canyonlike alleys, the ever-visible lemon sheen of the dome under which Our Shathra Anna resides and toward which nearly all the dirty alleys lead: the Atarite Palace. As an aide to Chancellor Blaine, as a very minor doer of the sort of work Our Shathra may not sully her hands with, I was going home again—even though Gabriel Elk and I would not set foot within several city squares of the domed palace. We were going among the poor, "the Mansuecerians themselves," Gabriel Elk would say, and our way was through the torch-lit sidestreets.

We were walking our horses. Their hooves clacked on the stones, their eyes were round with a mute claustrophobia, their nostrils quivered with the pungent smells of packed-in humanity. But we met no one in the streets. It was the time of the Halcyon Panic (hence, my assignment to Elk, whom the Magi feared as a potential demagogue), and at night everyone stayed docilely indoors—everyone but those with state business and, of course, the maddeningly uncoercible Gabriel Elk who had come on business of his own.

"Do you know where we are?" I asked him, a bite in my voice.

He halted his shaggy animal and looked at me. The old man's eyes were a pale green, his face as heavy as carven marble, the jowls giving way only slightly to his sixty-three years. Great white sideburns framed his cheeks, and his hair fell in bearish curls over his forehead and neck. "On Earth my sixty-three years would be seventy-five," he had told me when I was first assigned to him, but he carried himself with an intractable agelessness. In this alleyway in Lunn he looked like a statue that has willed its limbs to move, that has broken out of stone into life.

"I know where we are, Ingram. This city was mine long before you entered either the service of Our Shathra or the elitist gangs of Chancellor Blaine. Some say the Chancellor got his roan tooth by sucking blood up through it, and, from what I see, a bit of that blood is yours, Master Marley. You're as bumptious and ticky as a person of power."

"I work for persons of power, Sayati Elk." Against Blaine's wishes, Our Shathra Anna had given Gabriel Elk the title *sayati* in his fifty-sixth year, after the construction of Stone-lore and the presentation of the first series of neuro-dramas. In the seven succeeding years Blaine and the Council of the Magi had agitated quietly for the revocation of Elk's royal dispensation to assemble the people and for the nationalization of the formidable power complex he had built in the upland arena.

"So you do, Ingram, so you do. And in your own way you also are a person of power."

"I do what I must—to insure that the Halcyon Panic doesn't break out roaring in the throats of our within-doors maskers."

"And I do what I must, Ingram, to insure that when the 'maskers' come out to Stonelore they perceive an order in things which the universe and the Magi of Ongladred don't always choose to grant them. The order is there, it inheres, and I'm the man who reveals it to them."

The Shattered Moons moved in a yellow band beyond the in-leaning rooftops, a monochrome rainbow in the night sky. Only the brightest stars were visible behind it, and it was hard to imagine that Ongladred was an island besieged, that the culture we had twice before built up over six thousand years as colonists on Mansueceria was in danger of collapsing again, collapsing completely.

The street was silent; my voice echoed in it. "And so to give the maskers order, you've come tonight to buy a dead man."

"Not exactly, Ingram. I've come to buy a dead woman, a beautiful girl killed by reivers. And the order I try to give the Mansuecerians, the gentles, is a glimpse of the order inhering outside themselves—for inwardly they're disciplined, Ingram, they're more serene, more in control of the animal in themselves than you or I. Only artists have to rage, artists and rulers."

"Our rulers don't rage, Sayati Elk."

"No, they simmer, Ingram. The worse for them." His horse, a woolly beast, lifted its head, whickeringly barked. The old man pulled the horse's head down and began walking again. The stones rang. Shadows wrapped themselves around us like voluted capes. "My sense of direction never faileth," he said after a while. "Look there."

We had come to a side-canyon, a narrow crevice between two rows of maskers'-houses perpendicular to the alley by which, on the city's southeastern outskirts, we had originally entered Lunn. There was no room for our horses here. But I looked where Elk was pointing and saw a green-gowned figure on a third-story balcony on the lefthand side of the alley, a figure stooping beneath a pair of conical lanterns to see us. But for this solitary revenant and those two lanterns, the "street" was unhaunted, dark, and coldly daunting.

The Halcyon Panic had begun to play in me; I wanted no part of Sayati Elk's sinister purchase of a dead girl.

"Come on, Ingram," he said. "We'll tie our horses here." He wrapped the reins of his animal around a stone gutterspout; I did likewise. Our footfalls reverberating in the night air, we walked through the alley between the maskers'-houses. There was a balcony across from the one on which the stooping figure stood, and it seemed to me that it would require very little effort to step from the lefthand balcony to the righthand one, three stories' worth of darkness gaping beneath that step.

"Who's up there?" I asked.

"Josu Lief, the father of the dead girl. Or so I'd guess."

The man on the balcony called out. Before he called, I had not been certain that he was a man; the gown had confused me. It was mourning garb. Under him now I could see that the gown and his shaved head—he was newly bald—were his only concessions to "grief." The Mansuecerians are immune to it, genetically serene, philosophically spartan. "Sayati Elk?" Gentleman Lief called out. Then: "Please come up, both of you." A serene, spartan voice

We entered the bleak doorway. We climbed the corkscrewing stairs. We let Josu Lief usher us into a three-room apartment where the rest of his family, dressed in forest-green mourning gowns and sitting in the candlelit central chamber, awaited us. There were introductions. Lief's wife wore her hair cut short, as did the two female children. Josu and his young son were bald from the razor. They accepted the news that I was a minor official of Our Shathra Anna's oligarchy with utter blandness; they were maskers, and I was a nouveau Atarite, programmed to rule. Gabriel Elk was of them, but different; a throwback in whom the primeval aggressions still roiled, still threatened eruption. The old man was the bridge between the Lief family and me.

"Where's Bronwen?" Gabriel Elk asked.

"Through here," Gentleman Lief said, and led us out of the central chamber into a sleeping room where there were six pallets on the floor. The girl lay on the pallet on which she had undoubtedly slept while alive: Bronwen Lief, eldest daughter of these anonymous maskers. One family amid a city full of similar families, all of them de-beasted, shaped in their genes toward a civilizing harmony. On them had been founded the state of Ongladred; only rulers and artists raged, and we Atarites so seldom as to suggest an innate serenity akin to that of the maskers.

"Will you accept my price?" Elk asked Lief.

"I accept it, Sayati Elk."

"Good. The money has already been credited to you. It's there for your use. Three days from now, bring your family to Stonelore."

"And she will perform?"

"A special performance, for the Lief family and some privileged others. Not a neuro-drama, but a kind of reading."

"Will she later act in the dramas?"

"Such is my hope."

The three of us looked at the dead Bronwen Lief—her father with an expression predictably neutral, in which there was neither pride nor remorse nor pity nor anything paternal in a strictly Atarite sense; Gabriel Elk with quiet appreciation; and I, the outsider, with an awareness of terrible loss. For Bronwen Lief, arranged on her pallet in her white death-gown, was an image that called up evocative names: Helen, Guinevere, Ligeia. She was beautiful, but there was something in her young face hinting at the ability to betray; in a Mansuecerian, a masker, that look disconcerted, it slept in the corners of her mouth like an incongruous smirk, an anomaly of character. As a dirt-runner I had long ago learned to recognize such telltale glimmerings under men's false, placid exteriors. But Bronwen Lief was a masker girl, and a corpse, and the candlelight made her flesh resemble porcelain.

Gabriel Elk said: "I'm very pleased, Gentleman Lief. She's beautiful; she's what I'd hoped for."

"Our thanks, Sayati Elk."

I said: "How did she die, exactly?"

The two older men turned their faces toward me. Josu Lief, I saw, could not have been more than forty; even with a shaved head he was a handsome man, with full lips and dark eyes. "I have told our friends, in a fall. But there's more, as Sayati Elk knows. Last night she went with a young man, the one selected for her, to see the bonfires by the eastern channel, the bonfires holding off the sloak—"

"You let them go?" I said. "At this time?"

"Bronwen did as she wished. It wasn't for me to permit or hinder her, either one. She had a good life, Master Marley."

"And a short one. What happened on the coast with her young man?"

"Laird and she was walking in the rocks, looking toward the Angromain Archipelago where your renegade ancestors kill each other and catch fish, Master Marley. They was thinking on the cycle of the sloak and the barbarians way out to sea there. Bronwen's young man says they spoke of the bonfires on the beach and of living to oldsters in Lunn, such things as that. Then they saw an empty boat, just a pinnace, beached in a rocky place between two of the bonfires. No sooner had they seen it than they heard voices, men speaking in accents not of Ongladred. The men surprised them, a party of three or four thick-bearded Pelagans on a raid of some sort. The Pelagans ran at them, pushed Bronwen and young Laird from the rocks, and leapt to the sand. It was a short drop, Laird says, but Bronwen must have twisted her neck. Laird fell into a gravelly place and broke his leg. He shouted so the bonfire tenders on both sides come running, you know, but it was too late. Out to sea the Pelagans went, oaring it like madmen or fiends—and Bronwen was dead. And so she came home to us, and we dressed her like you see her. In her death-gown."

"And Laird?" Gabriel Elk asked.

"He's on the mend, I'll wager."

ii

We went back into the apartment's central chamber. The women sat on straightbacked chairs, doing something to the patterned quilts in their laps. Lief's son, his bald head shining, was on the floor marking a piece of paper with a stylus; he was about six.

"At least your boy won't be called up," Elk said. When the Halcyon Panic broke, military service for men between the ages of fifteen and fifty would be obligatory. Unless one were an Atarite (and in many cases, even then). I knew that inductions had already begun. Josu Lief confirmed me in my knowledge.

"They tapped me two days ago," he said. "I go in five days." And he would, too. Docilely, he would take off his mourning gown, don a warrior's breeches, and cover his shaved head with a leather cap. Then off to the Lunn garrison for his assignment. The masker, the gentle, would become a soldier—pacific in his innermost soul, but ruthlessly obedient in war.

"Then Gareth will be touched soon, too," Elk said, and genius or no he could not keep the regret out of his huge, corrugated brow. Unlike the serene Gentleman Lief's, his feelings toward his children—his child rather, now his only son—ran deeper than stoic affection. After all, Gabriel Elk was a mistake, an artist; in all things he raged, he harkened to a gong inaudible to maskers and Atarites alike.

We sat down. Gentlewoman Lief left her chair, went to a cabinet in the apartment's kitchen, and returned with three cups of *haoma*. This is a mildly intoxicating drink distilled from the bullcap fungus and banned at court; the maskers believe that it induces righteousness and piety rather than drunkenness. Curious, I sipped what was given me. Simultaneously sweet and tart, the haoma seemed to transfuse warmth through the lining of my stomach, into my veins and marrow, like a flow of heated blood. While Gabriel Elk and Gentleman Lief talked, I nodded and tried to heed their words.

"When will the Halcyon Panic break?" the old man asked.

"Not yet, Sayati Elk, not yet."

"Your neighbors?"

"They continue calm. There's talk of the sloak, and of the Pelagans, and even of the rupturing of the sun—but no one screams in his sleep, no one's yammering of Ongladred's death. Our Shathra Anna watches over us. She's a wise-eyed lady, wise in her watching."

Gentlewoman Lief smiled at her husband, the girls continued sewing, the boy colored his scrap of paper without heeding his father's visitors at all. At court, a young official's death would have kept us from secular activity for at least a day or two; here, it required all my haoma-ridden powers to remember that Bronwen Lief lay dead in the next room. Haoma. No doubt Josu Lief had had the examining physician administer an undiluted extract of the principal drug in this beverage to his daughter's corpse, as a temporary preservative. And here I was, embalming myself in a maskers' drink. Bronwen's face, her ambiguously smiling face, floated into my mind, into my sight. I gripped my chair.

Unaffected, Gabriel Elk was standing. The other people in the room began rising, too. I heard Josu Lief say, "Do you want me to bring her out to Stonelore tomorrow, Sayati Elk?"

"Have you a blanket you can spare?"

"I've finished this quilt," Lief's wife said. "You may take it, if you like. For Bronwen."

"Good. I'll wrap her in it, and Marley and I will take her with us now. There's no need in your carrying her out there tomorrow, Josu."

I was standing now. Someone took the cup out of my hands. Josu left the room. He came back with his daughter wrapped in the quilt. I noticed that the silken quilt, a series of cream-colored squares, was embroidered around its hem with blue flowers, the kind that grow on the cliffs above the Angromain Channel. Bronwen's face was not covered; her black hair fell over Josu Lief's supporting forearm. I watched as the father gave her into the arms of Gabriel Elk, even though by rights I ought to have been the one to carry her.

"Remember," the old man said. "Come three days from now." Then, turning to me: "Ingram, let's go." I managed to get to the door, and to open it for the burdened-down old codger. The stairwell yawned beneath us. The family, but for Lief's son, crowded into the opening. I stood with my back pressed against the open door, cold seeping up to me from the street.

"The Light stay with you," Gentlewoman Lief told Elk,

"and the Lie die." That was their religion, the whole of it, conveyed in two gently spoken imperatives. The woman said nothing at all to her dead child, though I half expected her to. The girl had gone to the Abode of Song—despite the fact that maskers never sing during their lifetimes. Singing is an activity that lies outside their stoic code; indeed, outside their very natures.

Gabriel Elk was on the stairs. I looked back into the Liefs' main sitting room and saw the six-year-old boy standing there with a piece of paper dangling from his hand. He raised his blond, boyishly thin eyebrows a little.

"Goodbye, Bronwen," he said.

I reeled toward the stairwell, grabbed the railing there, and clumped groggily down the steps behind the old man and the dead girl he carried. In the cold street we found our horses and rode toward Stonelore and Elk's rock-capped residence. Bronwen Lief, wrapped in a quilt embroidered with blue flowers, lay doubled over the old philosopher/playwright's saddle, wedged between the pommel and his paunch, deprived of dignity. Lunn faded behind us, and the Shattered Moons danced. Our horses climbed powerfully into the dark of the countryside. Immersed in wind, my head began to clear.

iii

Even though Stonelore lay seven kilometers beyond Lunn, to the southeast, it was easily accessible by a road running from the capital to the fishing village of Mershead on the Angromain Channel. In the spring the maskers set up produce stalls and vanity booths along this road, and did a good business among the travelers and fishermen going between Lunn and Mershead. Since it was in the spring that Elk presented his three neuro-dramas of the year, he had no difficulty attracting maskers to fill his circular stone amphitheatre. But, on the night we rode back from Lunn with Bronwen Lief over Elk's saddle, the equinox was still a good Mansuecerian month away; consequently, the Mershead Road was deserted but for a company of lately inducted maskers, carrying antiquated Yorkley rifles, marching toward the beaches. (The Halcyon Panic had had its subtle grip on Ongladred for the whole of the winter.) A few of these men hailed us civilly as we rode by, then the darkness loomed up again, and abruptly Elk goaded his horse off the road and into unmarked country—a stony shortcut to his home in the rocks.

The ground, covered with short grass, seemed to swell up beneath us, the horizons to expand. I imagined that at any moment we would ride into peril; our horses would plunge from the sea-fronting cliffs, the withdrawing tides would carry us to the barren archipelagoes where our enemies lived out their hatred for us. —Instead, the horizons contracted again as chunks and blocks of stone began to rise up around us.

Finally we rode into the rock-walled upland arena in which the Stonelore amphitheatre had been built. The amphitheatre was white under the Shattered Moons, its broad plastic cap gleaming dully. To the left of the amphitheatre was the energy unit that provided the power for both Elk's house and the animation of the delicately programmed actors in his neuro-dramas; it squatted in the dark like an outsized toadstool.

In Lunn a similar but differently constituted unit powered the heating and cooling systems in Our Shathra Anna's palace, as well as the glass flambeaux in the corridors and bedchambers. Solvent from his early literary activities, wealthy from his share of booty taken from the Pelagans during the midcentury skirmishes in which he had served as a commander, Elk had bought the components of the energy unit with his own funds; then he had engineered its design and construction, engaged in covert talks with a Pelagan minister, and acquired enough fissionable material to keep Stonelore running for three hundred years. Later he had admitted— openly—making a reciprocal arrangement with a representative of the barbarians that Ongladred had held successfully at bay during the undeclared, midcentury hostilities.

Those days were gone. Elk was past the age of conscription, and he lived and worked beyond the means or the capabilities of the citizens whom his work "enlightened." Only Our Shathra Anna and the wealthiest of Atarites could challenge his lifestyle. Several days before, I had asked him about this. "How can you, one of the people, justify the way you live, Sayati Elk?"

"I don't have to *justify* anything, Ingram. Our Shathra Anna gave me the title by which you address me, and Stonelore grew up around me as the result of the efforts of my hands and mind. I dwell here, but I don't look upon a single pebble of this site as 'property.'"

I laughed. "You're just a caretaker?"

"No, I'm a creator. Transient as they are, Stonelore and the neuro-dramas are my gift to the civilization of Ongladred."

"A civilization now threatened," I reminded him.

"Exactly, Ingram. So I create the harder. A social order promoting social order, and nothing more, isn't civilization at all; it's a machine for maintaining the status quo. The Mansuecerians live as they must, the Atarite Court rules as it must—but I have to give shape to voices and forms lying outside your experience or muffled so close to you that you're blind to them."

"Why? In these times, to what purpose?"

"So that you can experience them. And so that I can live." He had started to say more, but bit his heavy lip and turned away.

Now we guided our horses to the right of the amphitheatre and dismounted in front of the house carven out of the rear wall of the upland arena: Grotto House. Gareth, Elk's son, came out to greet us; he took the horses and led them to shelter in a stable down from Grotto House. (The stable was an anomaly; it was made entirely of wood, and it could not be seen from the environs of the amphitheatre.) Holding Bronwen, I watched the boy go. He was sixteen, very nearly the child of his father's dotage—except that Gabriel Elk was a long way from senile garrulity; he struggled to contain his natural affection for the boy.

Gareth was his parents' last child. Two older sons had died in separate accidents, one drowning in the Angromain Channel, the other apparently the victim of a thief or Pelagan raiders, very like the dead girl in my arms. This was years ago. A daughter lived in Lunn, married to a masker with no more fire in him than any other of their kind. She did not like to come out to Stonelore. As for Gareth, he had his father's heavy face, and he was trying to grow a beard. It was coming out thin, red, and lugubrious-looking, but he persisted in a standing refusal to shave. Too, he had some of his father's spark: already he had shown himself skillful at hacking boulders into strange, sinuous shapes. Sculptures, he called them, although it wasn't always easy to tell of what. He said they were supposed to be trees, artwork designed to suggest the possibilities of growth.

"Come inside," Gabriel Elk said. "Before you drop her."

My arms *had* begun to ache. We passed through a heavy wrought-iron gate that blocked the entrance to Grotto House, a gate with old Spanish scrollwork in the iron; and then I followed the old man into the foyer of the rock house. Illuminated panels made every wall glow, and two rough corridors led out of the foyer to right and left. "Where do you want her?" I asked.

"In the programming room."

Bethel Elk came out of the righthand corridor to greet us. She took her husband's hand and said hello to me. She was as tall as I; her arms were bare in a pale-yellow gown. Without self-consciousness she also wore a thin wire brace as additional support for her back, which she had long ago injured in a fall. She was a Mansuecerian, but it was rumored that her father had been an Atarite. How else account for the saucy cast in her eye, a look heightened rather than dampened by her age?

"The girl's beautiful," she said.

"Aye," Gabriel Elk said. "So I bought her. Now if Master Marley'll escort her down to the programming room—"

"Tonight?" the woman said. "Let her lie in a bedchamber."

"I'm going to work tonight," Gabriel Elk said. "Haomycin doesn't hold forever, my lady, and we have company in three days. Go on, Ingram."

I said: "Surely you can begin in the morning and still get done."

Elk grinned; his sideburns stood away from his smile like white wings. "Ingram's on orders to watch me," he said, "and he's too tired to do it. Don't worry, Ingram, I'm not going to sneak off while you're sleeping and file for citizenship among the Pelagans. Take Bronwen down the hall. Then go to bed."

"Fine," I said. Alone, I went down the corridor to the left, all the way to its end, then halted in front of the elevator there. The door slid open. I stepped in. Humming, the elevator dropped us three or four meters to the programming room.

I carried Bronwen Lief into this chamber, placed her on a table, opened the silken quilt away from her, and stared at her gowned body and her noncommittal lips. Still, the ability to betray was there even yet, in death as well as in life she could betray. In the programming room, amid support consoles, minicomputers, oscilloscopes, and Elk's privately engineered neural-surrogate equipment, I associated Bronwen Lief with everything that was then threatening Ongladred's civilization: the barbarians of the Angromain Archipelago, the mythical sloak, Elk's own wayward genius, and, damn me for thinking it, maybe even the inflexibility of Atarite rule. Somehow Bronwen Lief was all of these things; somehow she embodied all the intangibles of the Halcyon Panic.

Weary, I left the programming room, found my own bedchamber on the upper level, and slept until the sun was high.

iv

All the next day I saw nothing of Gabriel Elk. However, there was a tunnel running from the programming room to the comp-center beneath the Stonelore amphitheatre, and I was certain that the old man, laboring alone, was preparing both the corpse of Bronwen Lief and the comptroller room itself for the special performance two evenings hence. I was of Our Shathra Anna's intelligence service, the Eyes and Ears of the Court, but I'd begun to trust Gabriel Elk—more, to respect him. He was too busy, too unconcerned with our petty preoccupations to try to elude me.

At midday I threaded my way through the rocks to the stable. In the barren paddock I found Gareth and the Elk family ostler, a middle-aged masker named Robin Coigns. He had been sleeping when we arrived from Lunn the previous evening, and Gareth's father had chosen not to disturb him. Gareth, as usual, was chiseling at a block of stone on a split-rail table, and Robin was grooming Gabriel's horse, pulling out long strands of kinky sorrel hair. The other animal was beneath the wooden awning, eating.

I entered the paddock. "Hello, horsesweat," I said to Robin.

Blandly, the ostler grinned. Gareth was too busy to do anything more than nod. His chisel glinted in the anemic sun; splinters flew away from his gloved hands. This statue, this "tree," was going to be as convolute as any he had ever made. I shielded my eyes and looked into the sun, into feeble old Maz.

"Well, Robin," I said. "What do you think? Is Maz going to nova, blow up in Ongladred's skies? Everything else imaginable is supposed to happen when the Panic breaks."

"Maz won't blow," Robin said. "I'll expect the sloak first."

"Do you believe in the sloak?"

"It's been ver-i-fied, hasn't it, Master Marley?"

"Postulated, not verified."

"Well, Our Shathra Anna says there's geo-logical ev-i-dence."

"Some." I was always amused by the gullibility of maskers, particularly uneducated ones like the ostler Robin Coigns.

Gareth looked up from his work. "I believe in the sloak," he said. His wide face glistened with sweat; his patchy beard outlined his jaw with a moist, plastered redness. "And Father believes in it. As Robin says, there's evidence to support its existence—at least in theory."

"In theory," I said. I had heard all the arguments before. *Sloak* was the masker name for an apparently chimerical sea creature that no one had ever seen. No one had ever seen it because it dwelled kilometers off the coast of Ongladred, on the very bottom of the ocean floor: a millimicron-thin membrane of otherwise immense proportions cloaking the sea bottom all the way to Mansueceria's equator, where the planet's waters supposedly became too warm for so sensitive a monster. Legend had it that the sloak, which moved in slow, vaguely peristaltic undulations, thickened itself consciously every two thousand years and pulled its bulk over the entire surface of our island. Then, like a huge dappled eye, it lay basking, breathing, for a year or more, in the dull sunlight of our world—after which it returned to the marbled green depths of the Suthward Trench.

An unhurried, rhythmical departure, no doubt.

"Two previous civilizations on Ongladred died," Gareth said. "Died seemingly at the height of their glory; died without suffering human conquest. And Father says that it wasn't so terribly long ago—during or after the creature's last cycle—that the Angromain Archipelagoes were settled by fleeing Atarites. Only enough people survived on Ongladred to begin again. Ours is the third civilization of colonists so threatened, Master Marley."

"The sloak is an explanation only if you have no other," I said. "There's firmer evidence for two periods of mild glaciation. Why not accept these as the means of destruction you're looking for, Gareth?"

"Glaciation from the south!" the boy said heatedly. "Why accept the illogical? I prefer the sloak, Robin's sloak."

"The sloak it was," Robin said. "The sloak it was."

"And if the cycle holds true," Gareth said, "this is the year." With his chisel, he made several chips of stone fly.

"The more immediate threat to Ongladred is human, Gareth—the Pelagans. They're real, they're avaricious, and they've finally begun to demonstrate the unity to undermine us. Before, their own divisiveness kept them manageable."

"Ten thousand years ago, on Earth, the threat was always human," the boy said, chiseling, his brow furious. Then he halted, looked over the block of stone on the table, fixed me with his blue-green eyes. "And you, Master Marley, see a threat even in my father. That's why you've come to Stonelore. That's why we bed and feed you, one of the Eyes and Ears of Our Shathra."

"I do what I must." It seemed that I had used these same words a hundred times before. Ingram Marley, a dirt-runner, a spy with no cover. Robin Coigns finished grooming Gabriel Elk's horse and led it under the shelter; he began pulling the wire comb down the flank of the other animal, tactfully out of earshot. Aswim in a welter of ambiguous loyalties, I watched him.

"And so does my father," Gareth said. "He also does what he must, but you've placed him among the potential dangers to Ongladred. In reality he is in himself the culmination of what that civilization ought to stand for. Does the Atarite Court know what it's doing, Master Marley?"

"Do you question Our Shathra Anna?" I was ashamed to frame this response, but I didn't know what else to say to the boy; therefore, subtle intimidation.

He would have none of it. "Not Our Shathra Anna. She alone among you may understand what Gabriel Elk represents. It's Chancellor Blaine and the Magi of the Atarite Court whose wisdom seems to me suspect, Master Marley."

"How suspect, Gareth?" Then I asked him something else, before he could answer my first question. "Will you disobey your conscription order when it comes, as it surely will?"

"If Ongladred requires men to defend her, I will aid in her defense." The boy was indignant; his voice quavered. "My father fought for this island, and so will I. I, too, am an Elk, Master Marley."

"Your father's a man of influence. Will he let you go?"

"He would have to, wouldn't he? In everything, he obeys the laws of the island. Besides, he knows if he attempted to hinder me, I wouldn't be stopped; I would go without his consent." The boy's stare fell away from me, a gratifying respite.

Robin Coigns came back, his currying unfinished. He sat on a bale of fodder between Gareth and me; I was leaning on the paddock rail. Robin said, "They say all civi-li-zations die, Master Marley. It's the nature of things. En-tro-py, you know, all of it running down. But it seems to me, one way or the other, it can be fought, you know. So I'll fight it, too."

Apparently he had heard the last part of our conversation. I asked, "Are you of induction age, too, horsesweat?"

"Forty-nine," he said. "I'll go with Master Gareth. The top and the bottom of their numbers, we'll be. Youth and sa-gassa-ty."

Gareth laughed. I was grinning, too.

"Oh, I'm not worried a' tall," the ostler went on. "My father always said that at the third coming of the sloak, the Parfects would return, too. To watch over us, you know. They dropped us here six thousand years ago, he said, and they'd come back if things went too swackers, like they're starting to do now. Why, it's my opinion, Master Marley, that the Parfects are cruising a ship out there among the Shattered Moons right now, orb-it-ing, you know—watching over us Mansuecerians, the People Accustomed to the Hand. And maybe over you ruling Atarites, too, for governing us good like you have."

"Those are comforting notions, horsesweat. But I'm afraid your sloak and the hoped-for return of the Parfects are cut from the same mythical cloth; they cancel each other out. We're left with the Pelagan threat, and no mitigating circumstances."

"And don't forget the peril posed by my father," Gareth said.

My grin faded; then I saw that Gabriel Elk's son was baiting me, prolonging the moment of uneasy jocularity that Robin Coigns had given us. In the same spirit I said, "I won't. You keep reminding me. The children of geniuses ought to voluntarily slit their throats as soon as they're cognizant of their heritage—a gash in the Adam's apple. Otherwise, they begin to take themselves too seriously."

"You don't like my stone work, Master Marley? My trees?"

"You'd be better off petrifying driftwood. Wouldn't take so long, and the results would be about the same."

"That's a hit," Robin Coigns said. "That's a hit."

We talked some more, then went back through the garden of rocks to Grotto House. Bethel gave us haoma, biscuits, and jerky for a midday meal, and sat down to eat with us herself. It was the first time since I had been there that she had served haoma. The old man did not appear; it was doubtful that he had even slept that night. I thought for a moment of Bronwen Lief, of her disquieting beauty. Then I put her out of my mind and enjoyed the company of the Elks and Robin Coigns, the company and the food. The haoma began to work in me as it had done the night before in Lunn.

Afterwards I excused myself and retired to my bedchamber for a nap. I didn't see Gabriel Elk at all for the remainder of that day. Nor did I see him the next. Nor the next—until late afternoon.

v

The Magi at the Atarite Court had determined that if we on Mansueceria converted our system of time-keeping into Earthly terms, it would be the year 12,500 A.D. Of course, this was an approximation. We measured time not in this long-ago-discarded way, but in terms of how many Mansuecerian years had passed in the reign of our current shathra. The winter and spring of the Halcyon Panic were preternatural seasons in the Year 35 of Our Shathra Anna, and ensconced in Gabriel Elk's house at Stonelore I wondered how many more years she would reign. I hoped it would be many; she was an estimable woman.

As Robin Coigns had said on the morning after Elk's and my return from Lunn, there had been colonists on Mansueceria for six thousand of our years. We had been brought from Earth in starships conceived and constructed by a neo-human species whom our earliest records had always referred to as the Parfects—principally because Earth's last men had considered them free of all human vices, cleansed of the quasi-mythical taint of Original Sin. It was the Parfects who had saved mankind from ultimate extermination in the terra-cotta city of Windfall Last in the Carib Sea; who had re-deemed us genetically, providing for two contrasting but complementary types of individual (the stoically disciplined Mansuecerians, or "maskers," and the more aggressive, more emotional Atarites); and who had then delivered this popu-lation of half a million to the rugged heartland of Ongladred, on a planet more than eight hundred light-years from Earth. Another chance. Yet another chance, in an isolation even more splendid than that the ambient sea had insured at Windfall Last. Then, the early records and later legends unanimously agreed, the Parfects themselves had left us, gone back to turn all of Earth into the gardens of Adam's first paradise. As for man, he had the rocks of Ongladred— and another chance.

And for six thousand years, despite two major collapses, we had maintained ourselves entire; more, we had managed, with very few exceptions, to maintain our genetic heritage as well, the People Accustomed to the Hand and the People Touched by Fire alike. Together, we had survived. Now Atarite barbarians from the sea-blasted, storm-scoured archi-pelagoes in the Angromain Sea threatened all we had built together, and there were rumors in the land of the coming of the slow, ravening sloak and the imminent explosion of woe-beset Maz. It was the Year of the Halcyon Panic, as well as Year 35 of Our Shathra Anna; a self-conscious calm prevailed.

Late in the afternoon of the third day after our return from Lunn, Gabriel Elk emerged from his seclusion and greeted me in the open courtyard in the center of his house.

My ankles crossed, I had been sitting on a stone bench watching Maz drop mauvely down the sky. "How have you been faring, Ingram?" the old man said. His green eyes looked tired; his great, winged sideburns were unkempt, and I could see the previously muted resemblance between him and Gareth. For the first time, I could see it clearly.

"Well," I said. "And you? Are you done?"

"Done. I had to be. Tonight the Liefs are coming, Ingram, and some others."

"What others, Sayati Elk?"

"Be patient, and see." He stood in front of me for a moment, casting his long shadow over both the flagstones and my legs, then turned and went back into the house. I had to pull myself up and follow. I felt uneasy. I could sense all the diverse strands of my anxiety preparing to knot themselves together.

There was no supper that evening, no haoma to share. Bethel met her husband in the foyer, took his hand, nodded vaguely at me. Then we left Grotto House and walked across the sandy arena which the Stonelore amphitheatre completely dominated. Instead of entering Stonelore, however, we took up sentry positions in one of the natural doorways in the rock wall overlooking the Mershead Road. The wind blew balloons of sand out over the grass, Gabriel and Bethel talked in low voices, and I waited. Just waited.

At last the Liefs came, man and wife, distant figures walking on the low road; they had walked the seven kilometers from Lunn. Even after we saw them, it took a good while for them to reach us. Maz had set, and when they arrived the five of us stood in the twilight like liquid ghosts.

"Hello, Josu," Gabriel Elk said. "Welcome, Rhia. Tonight you'll see your daughter reanimated, given a kind of life again. Bethel will take you into Stonelore and show you your seats. I'll follow in a while. There are others whom I'm pledged to greet."

The Liefs went off with Bethel in the liquid dusk, toward the amphitheatre. When I looked after them, I saw Stonelore's broad circular cap glowing a soft yellow-orange. In response to my questioning look, Gabriel said, "Gareth's in the comptroller room. Tonight, he does my work." We turned again to the Mershead Road. Overhead, the Shattered Moons were scarcely visible, as milky as a thousand clumsily shaped pearls floating between Ongladred's strong rock and the heavens' weak stars.

At last we saw the vehicles on the roadway, and I knew that our visitors were Our Shathra Anna, her Chancellor, and some Atarite retainers—guardsmen. Two chariots preceded Our Shathra's equipage, and torches burned in the hands of the men in the chariots. The sound of the horses' hooves grew steadily beneath the sound of the wind, and Gabriel Elk and I watched as the chariots separated from Our Shathra's carriage and circled off in different directions, one halting about fifty meters from the gate in the rocks, the other undoubtedly taking up guard on the other side of the upland arena. The equipage, however, proceeded on up to us, black and silent, its matched horses caparisoned and haughty.

Gabriel Elk, waving his arms, directed the vehicle to the steps at the base of the amphitheatre. Robin Coigns had appeared from the darkness to help our eminent visitors get out and to show the coachman where he might shelter himself and his horses during the neuro-performance.

"Sayati Elk," Our Shathra Anna said.

The old man bowed, as did I. The carriage drew away from us. Arngrim Blaine, a tall, ascetic-looking man in his sixtieth year, smiled at us. Even in the failing light his roan tooth was visible, a translucent reddish-black canine pointing upward like a knife. Long ago he had had it scrimshawed with his initials (it was rumored), but over the years these had either faded or worn away (if they ever existed). He was a well-meaning, narrow-principled man. "Hello, Ingram," he said. "Sayati Elk. I'm happy enough to greet you, but not at all convinced that this trip was merited. Stonelore has always seemed a frivolous waste to me, and now more than ever."

"Arngrim has no taste for the arts," Our Shathra said. She wore a black cloak that fastened at her neck; although she smiled, there were grey circles under her eyes.

"Neither did Cyaxares of Mede," the Chancellor said. "Nor Walpole of Augustan England. Besides, Ongladred wasn't made for art."

Our Shathra Anna said, "With which man do you compare yourself, Arngrim—the Median king or the English minister?"

"The minister, Lady. The other would be presumptuous." He bowed.

"Art is an enrichment granted those cultures deserving it," the creator of Stonelore said. "Or inflicted on those attempting to repress it."

Our Shathra Anna looked at Gabriel Elk. When she spoke, her tone was liltingly sharp, ironically humorous. "Blaine is irritated because he can't rule in all things. Most of all, he can't rule me. I've come to see your entertainment, Gabriel, because I may not be able to come again."

"The season's dangers ought to have dissuaded us from coming tonight," Blaine said. "Two chariots! An inadequate guard, Lady."

"Then I love the lady for the dangers that she's passed," Gabriel Elk said. "And I welcome you both. Let's go inside." He didn't bow; his gallantry derived from conviction. Taking Our Shathra Anna's arm, he escorted the lady up the stairs to the wide illuminated portal of the amphitheatre. Chancellor Blaine and I trailed them up the steps, two serving-men, each as much a dirt-runner as the other—a situation which I found satisfyingly amusing.

Two of Gareth Elk's tree-sculptures flanked the wide door.

Inside, Elk led us to a glass booth on the theatre's highest circular tier, a booth reserved for Ongladred's Atarites and Atarite retainers. The top of the booth was open, and even though we were on Stonelore's uppermost level, the ceiling arched over us like a miniature sky, utterly out of reach. Our chairs were velvet-upholstered wingbacks set so that we could look comfortably down into the neuro-pit. Across from us, in the preliminary dark, we could discern Bethel Elk and the Liefs sitting poised and expectant on the continuous stone tier. Otherwise, Stonelore was empty—but sentient, immense, and brooding. Gabriel Elk had infused it with something of his own character.

"Those are my actress' parents," he said. "I felt that they should be here, too, if they wished to come."

"Of course," Our Shathra said.

"I hope," Blaine said, "that they're maskers in every sense, inured to feigned emotions and resigned to their daughter's death. This sort of thing can undermine even the stolidest personality, Sayati Elk."

"It hasn't yet, Chancellor. Tonight, in any case, a reading only. The neuro-drama doesn't undermine anything; it offers release, purgation, for a people manufactured to think they don't require it, but subliminally craving it in any case. The neuro-drama illuminates our oneness, it strengthens the social order you represent."

"When it's comprehensible, perhaps," the Chancellor said. "Mostly, at Stonelore, it criminally drains energy reserves." It was not impossible to admire the roan-toothed old pragmatist; even genius left him unabashed, wittily clawing.

Gabriel Elk answered him angrily: "The reserves are mine, not the state's! And the drain is far from criminal since the law refuses to permit human actors. Stonelore is a compromise with that law, Chancellor Blaine—a law of Atarite urging which you capably championed before the Magi. Perhaps you remember?"

"Very well, Sayati Elk, very well."

Our Shathra Anna leaned forward in her engulfing chair. "May we begin now, Worthies? These things are past argument and I've come for intelligent entertainment, not debate."

"Certainly, Lady." Gabriel Elk left the booth.

Chancellor Blaine turned to me. "Well, Ingram, what can you say for yourself? It seems you've been enjoying a vacation from the Court, a holiday at Stonelore."

"Shame," Our Shathra said. "You wanted him to come out here, Arngrim. Now you scold him for doing your bidding."

I said, "Anyway, I don't believe the old man is a threat to Ongladred; he'll precipitate no early break in the maskers' steadfastness, Chancellor—nor will the neuro-dramas planned for after the equinox."

Blaine asked, "What *does* Sayati Elk have planned, Ingram?"

"I don't know," I had to admit. "I'm not even sure what we'll see this evening, but Gabriel Elk's neither a fool nor an apostate."

"Thirteen days out here, Ingram, and you don't know what the man's planning. You're arguing from faith." Blaine's roan tooth seemed to slash at me. "When the Halcyon Panic breaks, when the maskers give themselves over to fear and misdirected anger and other inutile emotions, you'll find Ongladred's biggest fool and darkest apostate coexisting in the same skin, Master Marley: *yours!*" The Chancellor's thin lips drew together firmly, hiding the red-black canine.

"Melodrama," Our Shathra Anna said. "Your own fears betray you into rhetoric, Arngrim."

"I hope so, Lady," Blaine said, immediately calm again. "But I see no reason to court disaster. The neuro-drama is a folly, a corruption of masker and Atarite mores, that I can't comprehend your fondness for. In times like these, Lady, your protection of it—forgive me—seems almost perverse." He looked at me again. "In the meantime, Ingram, I think your mission at Stonelore is effectively at an end. Tonight you'll come back to Lunn with us."

"Very well," I said.

vi

Suddenly the neuro-theatre was plunged into absolute, impenetrable darkness. There was music: a single, stringed instrument playing mournfully. The sound—not loud, but resonant and golden—seemed to issue from everywhere at once. "At last," I heard Our Shathra's voice say, "the *folly* commences." Then a battery of incredibly bright lights threw their stinging yellowness into the sunken arena of the neuro-pit, Sayati Elk's "stage." Even yet, however, the blackness obliterated everything else in the Stonelore amphitheatre; we could not see Elk's wife and Bronwen's parents on the tier opposite us.

Then Gabriel Elk stepped into the light. As he spoke, he turned so that all in the theatre could hear him, even the phantom maskers whom he apparently imagined to be in the tiers above him. His foreshortened body, his monstrous hands, his upturned, expressive face all had a sharpness of focus intensified out of the realm of nature. Ageless he was, ageless and transcendent. Turning slowly, he spoke; and, without amplification, his voice reached out to us like a wave breaking. "My performer tonight is the corpse of Bronwen Lief, a girl killed by the Pelagans four days ago. I bow to her parents, for allowing me to buy her." He bowed in their direction. "What she will perform is not of my composition; indeed, it is not even of our tongue, and I have decided to let her speak it as its ancient poet, now forgotten, set it to paper. The strangeness of the language will be no stranger than the strangeness of our times. Ultimately, all languages are vehicles for the same remorseless, unending reaching out—even to the moment of man's extinction."

On that word he walked out of the neuro-pit, into the ambient dark. But he didn't return to our booth.

We were left staring into the neuro-pit. Then a section of the floor about three meters in diameter withdrew into the bowels of the amphitheatre; when it returned on its pneumatic lift-shaft, Bronwen Lief was standing on it—her supple body clad in a white Etruscan stola, her eyes reflecting back at us the disquieting glaze of her deadness. The music began again, livelier than before but still mournful. Just as the girl had no soul, the music now had no body; the thin plucked notes slipped away into the air. Perhaps Gabriel Elk intended for the music and the girl to complete each other, to make a whole human being out of an empty shell and a disembodied noise. I didn't know. This was the first time I had ever seen any sort of performance at all at Stone-lore; Arngrim Blaine enforced his own prejudices among the Eyes and Ears of Our Shathra Anna, and except for my assignment to Elk as a dirt-runner I might never have been permitted to receive the old sayati's special brand of "enlightenment."

The performance itself both bewildered and moved me. I saw a corpse behave as no living masker ever had, even under Atarite command in war.

Bronwen Lief, a dead girl, danced.

Maskers never danced—nor did Atarites, even though the range of emotions conducive to dancing lay well within our psychological compass. It was against the law. For the same reason that dancing was against the law, living human beings were forbidden to be actors.

As products of the Parfects' genetic engineering, the population of our planet reflected their unanimous verdict as to what qualities a reasoning creature ought to have. Out of the maskers the Parfects had bred avariciousness, aggressiveness, xenophobia, lust, and even a degree of the inclination to fear. At the same time the Parfects had recognized that survival in a new and hostile environment depended, at least in part, on these very "vices." Hence, they had engineered a second, smaller group of colonists to guide and administer to the first; these were the original Atarites, people in whom the dangerous dross of the animal, the primeval recourse to fang and claw, still had a bit of play—but subordinated now to the need to build, command, and protect.

The Parfects had even tried to program into our ancestors' genes and blood the elementary knowledge that the two groups were dependent on each other; that the seemingly irresistible urge to interbreed would lead to ruin; that the similar tendency for the People Accustomed to the Hand and the People Touched by Fire to go their separate ways, to take their own evolutionary roads, would have to be subconsciously, intuitively, fought. In all of this, the Parfects had perhaps demonstrated the extent of their own limitations. Still, we had managed to survive. Renegade Atarites had established themselves long ago on the islands of the Angromain Archipelago, and for several generations on Ongladred there had been more liaisons between ruler and ruled than were wise (my own grandparents were an example); but even so threatened and picked at, our civilization stood.

In Gabriel Elk's neuro-theatre I watched the dead Bronwen Lief go through the motions of a choreography programmed into her but seemingly motivated from within, from a *human* source. Of course, that source was Sayati Elk himself (and Gareth, too, for he directed some of the girl's movements from the comptroller room). The old man had turned technology into a kind of aesthetic, he had tried to infuse spirit into what was essentially a mechanical operation—not because he wanted to, but because he had to. The neuro-theatre was a compromise with the laws of Ongladred, a compromise that the old man could not have been entirely happy with. I was moved by Bronwen's dance because her programmer had come so close to accomplishing the impossible. She moved with genuine grace; her garment followed the flow of her limbs like a ghost counterpointing her motions. But, in reality, it was Gabriel Elk's vision, his need to communicate, that was flowing down there under the withering brightness of Stonelore's lamps.

Bronwen Lief was the vessel into which he had poured both vision and need. Because she was a corpse.

The law said that no human being could be an actor, no human being could take part in any sort of performance contrary to Mansuecerian nature. For uniformity's sake, the law included Atarites. The relatively high incidence of interbreeding between the two groups during the last century had made the law seem reasonable to many. An actor, after all, is one who constantly assumes roles requiring him to abase or repudiate, if only momentarily, the genetic characteristics given to him by the Parfects. One becomes something other than himself. Drama derives from conflict and emotion—excessive and aberrant emotion, according to men like Chancellor Blaine. In a society like Ongladred's, these men felt, such "artificial" emotions posed a very real danger to the persons acting them out; the audience for these spectacles was also in some danger of corruption, but a few of Our Shathra Anna's most influential Magi had deterred the closing of the neuro-theatre by arguing that it might be a healthy outlet for the subconscious turmoil of the ordinary Mansuecerian. Or maybe this was the rationalization of Our Shathra herself, who was a sympathizer, who enjoyed a slightly illicit entertainment. And so the issue of Stonelore balanced on the horns of the fuzzy moral ideologies of these two factions: One could attend Gabriel Elk's dramas, but one could not perform in them.

The dead, however, were exempt from the non-participation law. No stigma attached to the reanimation of corpses for actors; in Ongladred we had developed an almost callous disregard for death and the attendant luxuries of mourning, burial, and lingering memory—or at least the maskers had, out of both necessity and the hope for survival. Therefore, Sayati Elk reanimated the dead. He poured his vision and need into the only vessels the state would allow him, striving always to touch and transfigure. This he did for an audience that almost invariably sat mute and subdued to the end. That his audience again and again came back to be silently worked upon was his incentive to continue—that, and his obsession with a dream, and occasionally Our Shathra Anna's reaction, whether approval or pique.

Tonight she approved. "Beautiful," she said.

Mansuecerian dancer, Atarite applause—except that Arngrim Blaine made a sighing noise. He shifted his thin body in its chair and his lacy clothes rustled. I ignored the Chancellor. Leaning forward, I tried to catch every nuance of Bronwen Lief's performance.

Then it was over, or at least this preliminary part of it was. She came out of her last graceful pas seul into an equally graceful walk. Then stopped. She turned her eyes up to her parents, then faced in the direction of our booth and looked up at us. They were still dead, those eyes, still empty and glasslike.

The lute continued to play.

When she finally spoke, her voice was deeper than seemed right—but melodious. The ancient language in which she spoke came naturally to her lips and mesmerized us with its accents; we forgot our inability to understand and simply listened. From somewhere in the dark, his voice coming rich and assured after each line Bronwen delivered, Sayati Elk translated the forgotten poet's words.

The poem dealt with time, and with the inevitable crumbling away of empires, and with the poet's awe in the face of their passing. It dealt, too, with the nearly inconsequential prospect of his own death. A fluid poem with few pauses, and a headlong surging toward its final lines.

In Elk's translation we heard them:

> *And here face downward in the sun*
> *To feel how swift how secretly*
> *The shadow of the night comes on . . .*

Bronwen Lief folded her hands and let her head fall to her breast. And that was all; the show was over. A dance and a reading, with very little room for the sort of *emoting* Chancellor Blaine took exception to. Sayati Elk had programmed the girl and cautioned Gareth to underplay the "entertainment"; in everything but the subject matter of the reading he had aimed at conciliating my roan-toothed superior. Less than twenty minutes had gone by since the dimming of Stonelore's house-lights and the flaring of the great lamps around the neuro-pit.

Brevity had always impressed Arngrim Blaine.

vii

But afterwards, in the tapestry-hung dining chamber of Grotto House, we discovered that the poem's subject had not impressed him, except negatively. There were six of us around the great stone table there, and places for two more. Those two were for Gabriel and Gareth, acting now as our stewards, moving between dining chamber and kitchen with platters of food and decanters of vintage haoma. A silent masker woman, the cook and scullery maid Maria, helped them with these labors. Our Shathra Anna and Bethel Elk sat at opposite ends of the table, each as queenly as the other. To the right of Our Shathra, Chancellor Blaine voiced his objections to the reading while the Liefs remained humbly noncommittal.

He was saying, "I can only assume, Mistress Elk, that your

40

husband chose the piece we've just heard for its elegant pessimism. He must have had to rummage long and hard through your library—until he found a microchip whose very shape and color suggested the defeatism of its contents. A tasteless choice, considering the dangers besetting us now." He sipped the haoma from his cup, a small illicit pleasure.

"Or an appropriate one," Bethel Elk said.

"No. He might as well be a propagandist for the Pelagans. Suppose that this were given on the first night after the equinox. How would our maskers—" Blaine's lips tightened; he began again. "Forgive me. How would our *Mansuecerian* citizens react?"

"Why not ask the Liefs, Chancellor?" I said.

Husband and wife continued silent, Rhia smiling and Josu bland under his leather mourning cap.

Blaine went on: "You see, they can't yet formulate their reactions. But I believe the effect of a presentation like the one we saw tonight is bound to be insidious. And the neurodramas themselves are a thousand times more disquieting than Bronwen Lief's recital. Eventually, the people's faith in Our Shathra and the Atarite Court will be sabotaged." In the glow of the dining chamber's candles, his roan tooth glinted with carnelian highlights.

Gabriel and Gareth came in with baskets of potato bread. They were enjoying themselves. The old man smiled at his wife.

Our Shathra Anna said, "Arngrim is maligning your choice of material, Gabriel. Says you'll sabotage Ongladred and me with barbarian propaganda."

It was the boy who answered her. "Father will respond to that after we have eaten—if the Chancellor leaves anything for us." He and the old man went out again, and, surprisingly enough, Blaine smiled—wanly.

Then the Elks, father and son, returned and took up their

places at table with us. Gabriel spoke to the Liefs: "Well, what did you think? Tell me how you felt seeing Bronwen as you saw her." Unlike Chancellor Blaine, he genuinely wanted their reactions; I could see him preparing to take mental notes.

"I don't know, Sayati Elk," Rhia said. "She wasn't our girl, that one down there."

"Her voice, it was different," Josu volunteered.

"Getting the voice right is very hard," Gareth answered. "Father has to coordinate the neural impulses from the electrodes in Broca's area of the brain with the programming of the lungs, vocal cords, and lips."

"Why don't you just use a recording?" Blaine asked. "It seems to me you've made things unduly complicated for yourself, Sayati Elk."

The old man glanced at the Chancellor. He said nothing. He returned his gaze to Rhia and Josu. "Bronwen didn't sound like herself?" he asked.

Josu said, "No, sir. Not exactly—but it could've been that old sort of talk she was speaking in."

"Maybe it was the talk," Rhia said. "That different language."

"Which supports my contention that your choice of material left a good deal to be desired," Blaine said. "The language itself, Sayati Elk, alienated the Liefs from their re-animated daughter, whereas the moany business about every civilization crumpling into shadow certainly wasn't designed to send either Our Shathra Anna or me away from Stonelore happily whistling your praises. A bad choice—from a diplomatic point of view if not an artistic one, Sayati Elk."

"It's spoiled your digestion, not mine," Our Shathra told Blaine.

Suddenly there was a silence; a stillness descended on the dining room of Grotto House. Eight people stared at one another over the baskets of potato bread, over the decanters of haoma, over the silver platter of roast mutton and the bowls of bread pudding. A silence and a tenseness. Then Arngrim Blaine raised his cup and sipped. By this simple movement he directed our attention to him. Looking over the rim of his cup, he spoke to Gabriel.

"Is Ongladred going to die, Sayati Elk?"

"Probably. One day."

"Soon?"

"*Soon* is a relative term, Chancellor Blaine. On what scale do you wish me to apply it?"

"Bronwen Lief's performance in Stonelore suggested that collapse is inevitable. I'm supposing that you selected the piece out of some rational, therefore comprehensible motive? What motive? To frighten us? To warn us? To suggest that resistance to fate is foolhardy? What, Sayati Elk? As for my definition of *soon,* do you think Ongladred will die during our lifetimes?"

"It's conceivable."

"Is it inevitable?"

"Even its death isn't inevitable, Chancellor Blaine. Societies fall when their leaders fail."

A pause; a darker tension.

Blaine's mouth was open slightly; a thread of spittle lay across his discolored tooth. He sipped more haoma. Then he said, "Who do you see as failing first, Sayati Elk? The Atarite Court in Lunn or the wolfish Pelagan captains across the Angromain Channel?"

Gareth Elk, the boy, said, "Whoever is least flexible, Chancellor Blaine; whoever is least adaptable." It was a thought I had had before, but never voiced. Blaine himself, though capable of a quick and witty range in conversation, was not otherwise known for his readiness to abandon old ways, old prejudices. The boy, I felt, had inadvertently given voice to our most basic fears about Ongladred's time of trials—the suspicion, even among Atarites, that our leaders had lost the quality of vision.

Then Our Shathra Anna said, "We may have as much as a year before the Pelagans put us to the test, perhaps as little as three months. Right now they're content for reivers and fear-strikers to harass, to steal, and"—here she nodded at Rhia and Josu Lief—"to murder when surprised in these pursuits. Invasion is not yet. We have a little time to mobilize. Even so, Gabriel, you ought to remember one thing in particular."

"Yes, Lady?" he said.

"That you must include yourself among that group of leaders who may fail or not fail in the attempt to preserve Ongladred."

"I, Lady?"

"Come, come, Gabriel. You're too old to play coy. Just as Arngrim and I are"—she inflected her next word self-consciously—"*political* leaders, you're an intellectual leader of our island."

Chancellor Blaine almost smirked. "In other words, Sayati Elk, you have a responsibility nearly as great as ours."

"Sometimes," Bethel Elk said, "Gabriel views his efforts at Stonelore in a Promethean light; against a hostile array of gods and vultures, he labors alone for the redemption and advancement of humanity."

"Oh, no," the old man protested, grinning. "Not alone. The gods and vultures I don't dispute, but I've always had help—you, Gareth, and lately even tight-lipped Master Marley there. The labor's almost always been *intellectual*, though," he continued slyly. "I wouldn't presume to put my foot in *politics*."

The meal went better after that. I studied the ornate woolen tapestries on the walls; I enjoyed the haoma, the food, the less sensitive drift of our talk. It was difficult to believe Stonelore's relative isolation from the Atarite Court, the belligerence of the inhabitants of the windy archipelagoes, the nightmarish threat of a creature called the sloak. Candles flickered. The evening drew to a close, as did my own residence at Grotto House. Oddly, I regretted this fact; I didn't want to go back to Lunn.

Then Our Shathra Anna said, "Arngrim, you'd better tell the Elks of Gareth's conscription."

Talk ceased again.

Chancellor Blaine said, "The gist of it is that Gareth and your ostler—"

"Robin Coigns," Bethel said.

"Yes. Gareth and Gentleman Coigns must report to the Lunn garrison in two days. Our Shathra wished this message to come from me personally, Sayati Elk, not from an induction-runner."

"Two days!" Bethel said.

"That's very little notice," her husband added.

Our Shathra said, "The message was to have come a day or two ago, Mistress Elk, but we hoped that hearing it from our own lips would make the news less distressing. I'm sorry the notice is not more, though. Sincerely sorry."

Josu Lief put his arms on the table. "You'll be reporting, Master Gareth, when I do, it seems."

"That's fine with me," Gareth said. "The hardship's not mine, but Father's. He'll have to do all the work, virtually all the work, in the neuro-theatre by himself. Mother can't work in the comptroller room; her back won't let her."

Gareth's comment seemed to be a serendipitous clue for Chancellor Blaine; quickly he interjected: "Sayati Elk, we can offer you the command of a unit of recently inducted men—a naval unit—if you choose to accept now. You will hold it for a year, or until this crisis is past. Should you accept, spring performances at Stonelore will cease to be a problem for you. Gareth's absence won't be felt here."

"Certainly it will be felt," Bethel said.

Blaine qualified this comment: "I meant that your husband's work in the neuro-theatre wouldn't be impeded by his absence."

"Because there wouldn't be any work in the neuro-theatre," Gabriel Elk said. "I'd be captaining a contingent of young Mansuecerian seaman against the Pelagans—at sixty-three. Stonelore would close."

"Regrettably," Blaine said.

"I refuse." Gabriel Elk turned to Our Shathra Anna. "Lady, was this proposal of your own devising? Am I to understand that you wish me to close Stonelore and hobble off to war?"

"You are far from hobbling, Gabriel. But no. The proposal originated with the Chancellor himself."

"Who believes," Blaine said smugly, "your intellectual leadership can be put to good military use, Sayati Elk. Since survival depends on leadership."

"I refuse. I'm too old for conscription. I've served."

"Our Shathra Anna," Gareth said, rising, "I'd like to go tell Robin."

"Please. Go ahead."

As the boy left, Gabriel Elk said, "In any case, we've nearly finished. When you return to Lunn, Lady, I humbly request that you let Josu and Rhia share your coach. The roads are dangerous at night."

Our Shathra agreed, and in another twenty minutes our entire company was outside, in the shadow of Grotto House, under the motionful brightness of the Shattered Moons. The Stonelore amphitheatre loomed up before us like an immense round starship, promising us Earth. It was cool. We saw Gareth and Robin Coigns walking toward us across the upland arena, Our Shathra Anna's equipage rattling along behind them like a circus cage of noisy blackbirds. Somehow, the equipage struck me as an evil thing. Above the caparisoned horses the driver snapped his long whip; apparently they had not been unbridled during the whole of the long evening. A second time the driver snapped his whip, and a third.

In front of Grotto House, Josu Lief crumpled to his knees in the dust and then pitched forward on his face.

If I hadn't seen the spark of uncanny red in the rock spires opposite us, I would have supposed the man had fainted—but the three successive crackings of the carriage driver's whip had concealed the report of a rifle. The second shot had no such fortuitous cover, however, and the burst of fire from the rifle muzzle seemed terrifyingly brighter than the first one. The report and the ricochet were deafening.

"Get down!" someone shouted. "Get back inside!"

I fell to the ground and rolled. I saw the three women—who had come out last—duck back into the deep well of Grotto House's inset entrance. Gabriel Elk and Arngrim Blaine scrambled into the rock garden to the entrance's right. I rolled again. On my stomach once more, I looked up. Gareth and Robin Coigns, caught in the open, ran for the protecting curve of the amphitheatre; the carriage rattled after them, horses whinnying.

Another spitting of fire; another shot. Everything was noise and moving bodies.

At last I found some cover for myself, a crevice on the side of Grotto House leading down to the stable.

"Gareth!" Gabriel Elk shouted. "Gareth!"

"Here, with Robin!" the boy answered from the portion of Stonelore's wall out of our concealed enemy's sight. "We're all of us whole."

viii

For the first time all evening I was alone with my thoughts, blood revving through my temples, roaring in my ears. The Shattered Moons buckled, flowed, shifted in their myriad orbits. I tilted my head back against the rough wall of my hiding place and watched them.

I, Ingram Marley, dirt-runner and spy.

For three hours I had been subsumed in the personalities of people more important, more powerful, than I. Now, through this violence, I had been given back to myself. The gift wasn't entirely appreciated. Involuntarily my shoulders pulled up against my neck, my palms flattened against cold stone.

I wondered how long the lot of us had to live. If the armed men in the rocks had got past Our Shathra Anna's chariot guard, who remained to save us? Only ourselves: Gabriel

Elk and son, our effete Chancellor, Robin Coigns and the coachman, and one member of the Eyes and Ears of the Atarite Court. Stonelore and Grotto House lay too far away from either Lunn or the Mershead Road for us to count on accidental reinforcements—although if the court party were too long in returning, the Magi would dispatch a contingent of horsemen.

Two, three, four more shots sounded in Stonelore's arena. Could they be heard on the Mershead Road? Maybe. As dull, echoing *pings* over the sounds of wind and sea. It wasn't likely that anyone would follow them up.

Frozen in place, I felt my own impotence in the face of a reasonless, impersonal hostility.

Then the hostility took on a distinctly human character: there was laughter from the rocks opposite us. Gleeful, self-assertive laughter which even the wind couldn't drown with its gusting.

Then two more shots, ricocheting away.

Then still more laughter and a voice crying out, "Ilk! Ilk! You surrender!" After which the old man, from his hiding place with Blaine, shouted an obscenity. There was disconcerting silence then; no shots, no braying laughter.

Several minutes passed.

Finally the voice in the rocks began taunting us in a dialect both lilting and guttural, a dialect which I knew as Pelagan but which I had never learned. Our attackers—how many murderers peered down on us?—were men from across the Angromain Channel, reivers, thieves, fear-strikers, danger-drinking barbarians. I though of Josu Lief lying face down in front of Grotto House. In less than a week these randomly operating Pelagan agents had killed two members of the same family. And one of them, drawing down on us with a stolen rifle no doubt, was alternately laughing and spewing out streams of incomprehensible invective.

After a time I realized that the hidden reiver was declaiming poetry at us, venomous couplets in his own tongue. He wanted Gabriel Elk, Ongladred's only literary giant, to suffer these insults in a form that mocked the old man's genius. And so he railed away at us like an actor, disdainful both of Sayati Elk and of the Atarite law that had indirectly given rise to the neuro-theatre. More than likely, Chancellor Blaine was chewing his upper lip with chagrin, his roan tooth on the verge of breaking flesh. How must he feel, in a situation in which he was as powerless as I?

"Ilk! Ilk!" the reiver called out; then regaled us with brusque, barbarian couplets.

For answer the reiver got three bursts from a handgun and a bit of bravado from Arngrim Blaine. "You'd better get out while you can!" his thin voice shouted. "If you don't go now, you'll not make it!"

I couldn't see around the crevice containing me, I was afraid to look out—but apparently the old Chancellor had taken the handgun from beneath his cloak and fired in anger. Gabriel Elk, beside Blaine in the low rock garden, translated his message into the Pelagan dialect and added a severe-sounding message of his own. I realized then that my own fear was greater than Chancellor Blaine's, that it was my own weakness that had imagined *him* chewing *his* lip. I was afraid because we were pinned down in Stonelore's arena. Still, we were not automatically doomed to end up like Josu Lief, wavy pencils of blood outlining our chins and discoloring the ground.

In my belt was a knife, a dagger with an elaborate haft. Almost every Atarite or Atarite retainer carried one like it; mine, like most of the others, had never been used. I curled my fingers around the haft and edged away from the crevice's opening, my back still making contact with stone. Rock encased me. Then the crevice funneled out and the night sky seemed to flood in on me. A tattering of wind slipped through a smooth-worn hole in the granite passageway, and later two separate, fancifully carven windows looked out on the narrow path leading down to the stable. I pulled myself up and crawled through the larger of these.

On the path, I ran.

Almost at once I came to the fenced-in paddock in front of the horses' shelter, a stable without walls. Despite the moons and the attenuated starlight, it was dark here; every shape appeared distorted, angular, unreal. Above me, in the Stonelore arena, I heard more rifle fire, echoings of deliberately hysterical laughter, and the mocking lilt and clack of the reiver's "poetry"—all of this noise incredibly tinny with distance. It was a temptation to go on down the path, find my way to open country and tall grass, and circle back to Lunn. *To bring back help,* I said to myself more than once; *to bring back help.*

Instead, I opened the paddock gate and walked between bales of fodder that Robin Coigns had left out for his animals. Maybe he had come down here during our entertainments at Stonelore and Grotto House and carried a bale or two back to the arena for Our Shathra Anna's horses. If so, he hadn't returned to the paddock for a while.

One of the distorted shapes that I nearly stumbled over was not a bale of fodder; it was Gabriel Elk's round-eyed, woolly gelding. I knelt. A reiver had plunged his knife into the animal's breast and then ripped the blade upward toward the long, vitally muscled throat. The other animal, the one I had ridden to Lunn, had been dealt with similarly.

How many Pelagans had done this? What had happened to the chariot guard? Alone, I almost wished myself back with the others.

The smell of recently spilled blood, warm and salty, commingled with that of dry fodder and the horses' last, scarcely cold droppings. These things daunted me. I trembled with nausea and the night's chill. I heard Chancellor Blaine's handgun again; he could not have many shots left, unless he also wore ammunition under his lace cloak.

Why had the Pelagans not placed men on both sides of the Stonelore arena? Had they done so, those of us emerging from Grotto House would have had very little chance of getting either back inside or to cover. Maybe we had come out before they expected us to. Certainly they had been busy up until that moment. The chariot guard must have purchased a little time for us. After slaughtering the guards and our horses (our transportation down from Gabriel Elk's citadel), the reivers had crossed back to the other side to see what they could do with Coigns and the unsuspecting coachman. There could not be too many of them; otherwise they would have worked in several concerted, simultaneous assaults rather than in cautious stages. Like me, the Pelagans were amateurs—infinitely more daring and bloodthirsty maybe, but not inherently more competent.

I stopped wondering; I stopped thinking.

If I managed to get onto the roof of the stable shelter, I saw that I could pull myself from there to the top of the rock wall into which Elk had built Grotto House. The rock wall, though broken in one or two places, inscribed a rough circle around the Stonelore arena.

So I climbed. I stacked several bales of fodder, then attained the shelter's roof. Then I fought the wind and the dizzying sky and clambered onto a rectangular ledge projecting out over the roof. From there, up to the rugged dentition of the rock wall itself.

Using hands and feet alike, I edged my way between these granitic, Brobdingnagian teeth, through the sudden drops, and over a few treacherous flat surfaces—toward the chattering Pelagan who had murdered Coigns' defenseless horses and the masker Josu Lief.

Something very ancient had come awake in my blood.

At one point I realized that I was on the roof of Grotto House. A useless realization. The rooms lay embedded in the stone under me like fossils buried in strata geologically unapproachable. The tapestries in the dining chamber; the electric wall panels in the foyer; the sound of women's voices. I wasn't a part of those things anymore; I was alone, moving stealthily toward some indefinable but necessary end. The Shattered Moons accompanied me.

Halfway around the wall I did something stupid: I stood full up and looked down into the arena.

I saw Gareth and Coigns huddled beside the amphitheatre, Our Shathra Anna's equipage a tangle of reins and shadows and jittery horses in front of them. The ostler and Elk's son were gesticulating madly at the coachman; he was slumped down in front of his seat, warily keeping his head low. As I watched, they managed to attract his attention and communicate to him their wishes.

Then, in rapid succession, these things happened: The coachman nervously jumped down from the equipage. He threw open the door on the side away from me. Gareth and Coigns rushed out from the wall and hurdled into the coach, which began angrily rocking. The coachman, shielded by the amphitheatre, slapped at the flanks of the gaudily accoutred horses, shouted at them, tugged at bridles. First a lead animal, then one in the second rank, reared in their traces; then all four of them plunged forward together, yanking the carriage out of its angry rocking. The coachman jumped back out of the way and sidled to safety along the base of the amphitheatre's wall.

Rattling and churning, the equipage jounced toward the opening by which the Liefs and the Court Party had originally entered the arena. The two men inside had not a bit of control over where it went or at what speed, they simply kept their heads down.

One of the reivers fired at the departing carriage. I saw

him silhouetted on the wall's rim, upright among the rocks. We were almost on eye level with each other, though fortunately he didn't look my way. Fascinated, I remained where I was. I thought I could see another Pelagan crouched beside the first, staying out of sight: the profile of a hawklike head.

Because of the intervening bulk of the amphitheatre itself, the man with the rifle had only a moment to stop the carriage, that moment when it burst into view again on the other side. But by then the matter was out of the reiver's hands. Although not in full control of the situation, Gareth and Coigns had escaped. Our Shathra's horses, ears flattened and manes floating, hurtled toward the Mershead Road.

A shot from Arngrim Blaine's handgun reminded the armed Pelagan that he couldn't take aim with impunity. He slumped quickly out of sight, so quickly in fact that I thought he might be wounded.

I waited.

It was several minutes before the more articulate of the two Pelagans began taunting Gabriel Elk again. "Ilk! Ilk! You surrender! That coach going off, it means nothing!" Then the mocking couplets, a singsong of scorn. Arngrim Blaine responded; the old man translated. The old man shouted words that carried a taunt of their own. Back and forth, this colloquy of deprecation—and I began moving again.

No thinking, I told myself; *deeds only.*

In another ten minutes I had worked my way over a broken stretch in the wall and back into the gnarled rock. The voices of the Pelagans came to me more and more clearly; when the poet wasn't shouting his insults, I could hear their exchanged whispers and even the irregular breathing of one of the men. At last I could see them. I hugged a spire of rock behind their natural blind and tried to still the revving of my heart. Looking out over the grassy highlands surrounding Stonelore, I saw no sign of the chariot guard

who had supposedly taken up his watch there. The Pelagans
had so thoroughly dealt with him that the landscape might
have cracked open and swallowed him, chariot and all.

No thinking! With that, I leapt down into the reivers'
blind. Blood pounded viciously behind my eyes, rudely insistent. A face turned toward me, a face unlike any I had
seen in Ongladred.

The Shattered Moons poured light over the features of
that face and over the whole of the shape squatting to its
left. It was the shape to the left that had the rifle, I saw the
barrel glinting too late. That figure I should have attacked
first—not this unarmed one, not this odd, glowering mask
rising up out of its own off-balance surprise to confront me.

I could feel my fingers gripping the haft of my knife—was
dimly aware of the knife itself sweeping up in an arc to my
ear, the blade quivering briefly a forearm's length from the
face beyond it.

Then, not wanting it to be the way it was happening,
wanting a less terrible portion of the Pelagan's anatomy for
a target, I pulled my knife down into his face—stabbed
once—then drew back as the reiver screamed, clutched his
fearsome wound, and rolled away.

(An image of the dead horses flashed into my mind.)

My weapon clattered into the rocks.

As I had done a few minutes before, I stood there upright
and exposed, stupid in my immobility. The other Pelagan,
his odd face somehow managing an expression utterly incredulous, began to rise. He brought his rifle up, a rifle that
had been throwing off sparks and noise for over thirty minutes now, and all I could do was remark the clumsiness of
his effort and the way the barrel shone so prettily. Would this
thing kill me?

Then a shadow eclipsed the second reiver, knocked the
rifle out of his hands, and bobbed nimbly out of harm's way.

Old Robin Coigns, alias Horsesweat, had jumped into the blind and disarmed my would-be assassin.

A moment later Gareth Elk followed Coigns out of the darkness, and the three of us stood there looking down on the disarmed Pelagan. The one whom I had stabbed lay off to one side, dead or certainly dying, his face mercifully twisted away from us.

No one spoke. There was the almost peaceful sound of heavy breathing, together with a misleading glut of peaceful white moonlight. I was empty of whatever had moved me so violently to this place. A malarial dizziness still ran through my blood, but the infection itself was gone.

I looked at Robin Coigns, I looked at Gareth Elk, I looked at the disarmed Pelagan. They in turn looked at me.

ix

Back in the Stonelore arena we tried to piece the situation together.

Someone had wrapped poor Josu Lief in a blanket; the women were inside Grotto House, Our Shathra Anna and Bethel Elk senselessly comforting the dry-eyed, almost unperturbed Rhia.

In the arena, I had my first real opportunity to look at the man we had captured. He was bound. Too, since he had proven annoyingly voluble on our trip back to the arena in Our Shathra Anna's carriage, he was gagged as well. Gareth had used the man's shredded undertunic for both the binding and gagging. Now the Pelagan sat in the dirt beside the luminous amphitheatre while Coigns and the coachman tried to calm the horses, and the rest of us huddled together beside the dust-covered equipage, assessing and reassessing.

"Just look at him," Arngrim Blaine was saying. "He *isn't* a man. How can you argue that he's a man?"

"Despite his looks," Gabriel Elk said, "he's a man very much like you, Chancellor Blaine." He paused, then added sardonically: "Or me. But perhaps more like you since the people of the archipelagoes were all originally derived from Atarite stock, and I have to confess a background predominantly Mansuecerian. Nevertheless, Chancellor, the man's a human being, not an animal."

"Look at him, Sayati Elk! Look at him!"

I looked at the Pelagan captive. The Chancellor was over-reacting, as I had overreacted to my first glimpse of the face of the reiver I had killed. It was easy to see that our captive belonged to our species, although certain minor differences in physiognomy and anatomy made it possible to *pretend* an evolutionary breach had occurred.

Sitting in the dust, his knees drawn up to his chin, his head balanced sullenly there, the reiver was demonstrably human. His dark eyes followed us with the same pupil-bright disdain with which a minor court official might regard a nouveau Atarite like Ingram Marley: I knew the look. It was made bearable now by the fact that he directed it against all of us—Gabriel, Gareth, Blaine, Coigns and the coachman, as well as me. In the Pelagan's eyes, we were the subhumans, the creatures not deserving the name *Man*. He lifted his head from his knees and threw it back against the amphitheatre's wall.

These physical distinctions existed: The captive was darker than any of us; his hair hung straight and black over his forehead and ears. His upper eyelids had a tuck in them, an epicanthic fold, Gabriel said. In fact, the old man told us that the Pelagan's appearance would have once been termed at least quasi-Mongoloid. Contradicting this assessment, however, was the reiver's abundant body hair, a sparse, ravenlike down over hands, arms, and face, though so thin on our captive's face that only the moonlight and my own proximity made this hair visible; on the man I had killed this facial down had seemed more horrifying, the sort of animalization of human features that Blaine was now insisting upon. Earthly Mongoloids, Elk said, had very seldom had a great deal of hair on their faces and bodies.

Finally, our captive had a purplish patch of skin on his throat, distinctly visible now because his head was back.

"All the people of the Angromain Archipelagoes don't look like this one," Chancellor Blaine said. "I know they don't, I've had distasteful dealings with a few of them before."

"The man I killed had similar features," I said. "Face, body hair, all of it."

Gareth affirmed this. We had left the dead man in the rocks, not wanting to sully Our Shathra's carriage any more than was needful. "He even had a mark on his throat like this one."

"From what I've heard and seen," Gabriel interjected, "this type—this quasi-Mongoloid type of individual—isn't at all uncommon in the archipelagoes now. I've had dealings with the Pelagans many times, Chancellor—more often than even you have, I'd imagine—and I've seen men resembling this one more than once. The Pelagans esteem men like him," nodding toward our captive, "because they seem to be particularly daring and resourceful. Many like him are in positions of leadership."

"Do they also esteem them murderous and cruel?"

"Life in the archipelagoes is not entirely like life in Ongladred, Chancellor; values differ."

"Obviously."

"There weren't many Asians among the final population of Windfall Last," I said. "Were there?"

"No," Gabriel Elk said.

"Then why should a people who look like Asians—the tuck in the eye, the dark hair, the yellow-brown skin—suddenly appear out in the Angromain?"

"It hasn't been all that sudden; it's been incremental, Ingram—though what the precise origins of people like these are, I don't know. Maybe the Parfects *engineered* an Atarite heritage into the genes of some of those penultimate Asians in Windfall Last." Gabriel Elk, something of an engineer himself, here pronounced the word with a deliberate nasality. "The descendants of some of these individuals were undoubtedly among the Atarites who fled Ongladred a millennium ago. Ironic, yes?"

"How do you mean, ironic?" Blaine asked, visibly peeved.

"Many of the oldest Earth civilizations were Eastern. Now, out here, eight hundred light-years from our spawning place, Oriental physical characteristics are asserting themselves again."

"But altered," I said.

"Yes," the old man agreed. "Altered. As everything alters, as everything changes—except ourselves." Nobody said anything to that; the comment had a self-consciously sagely ring to it that Elk usually avoided. Moreover, the Parfects' grand experiment on Mansueceria didn't altogether support the concept of an unchanging and unchangeable human condition. Long ago, for our own good, we had been "engineered." No one could dispute that.

We were all beginning to feel the length of the day, the late-evening cold, the after-numbness of fading shock. We moved around in the arena's dust; we watched Coigns and the coachman soothing the sweaty-flanked horses, currying them with rags, talking to them; we tried to shake ourselves back into reality with random gestures and banal resolutions.

The reivers had murdered the chariot guards, just as I had earlier assumed, and the chariots' horses had more than likely pulled the empty vehicles all the way back to Lunn. This was something none of us had come to grips with yet. As was the death of Josu Lief. Coigns put the dead masker, wrapped in a borrowed blanket, into the equipage—on the seat opposite to the one on which Chancellor Blaine and Our Shathra Anna would ride.

Blaine raised no protest.

Then we all came back to our captive, the Angromain barbarian who had taken part in, perhaps even masterminded, the night's surreal carnage. The women remained in Grotto House, waiting for us to do something, regal in their patience; and at last all our movements came to revolve around the sullen, insolently watchful Pelagan who had very nearly killed me up on the rock wall.

Out of this uncertain numbness Gabriel Elk said, "Take the gag out of his mouth."

The coachman did so, stepping away as soon as the cloth was free. A film seemed to pass over our captive's eyes, he shuddered, his body feebly radiated its weariness.

Then the man began to curse us. He cursed vehemently, moving his head from side to side against the wall.

Gabriel Elk grabbed my arm and raised his voice over the belligerent cursing, "This is the other one, Ingram. No style, no subtlety. You killed the poet, the one with the flair. Did you know that?"

"Not until afterwards."

"Are you glad?"

"No," I said. I pulled my arm away. "Why should I be glad? Why should I be glad either way?"

The Pelagan stopped cursing, drawn to our disagreement. Gabriel Elk ignored him; the old man's eyes, amid leathery

wrinkles, looked into mine with an intense and unsettling con-
centration. "You shouldn't," he said quietly. "You shouldn't
be glad, Ingram. Forgive me."

"I don't know why I did what I did," I said. "I'd never
killed a man before. Something happened to me."

"Never mind that now, Ingram," the old man said. He
turned to his son. "He's run out of curses for the moment,
Gareth; while he's quiet, put something on his wound. Clean
it out first."

The boy moved to do his father's bidding. Arngrim Blaine
said, "We needn't let our humanitarianism run past the cup's
lip, Sayati Elk," but his voice carried no real rebuke and he
didn't try to impede Gareth's bandaging of the captive.

The captive himself clenched his teeth while Gareth
worked at his shoulder, but kept his eyes suspiciously on the
boy, now and again letting them rove to our faces as well—
where they seared their suspicion and disdain into our flesh.
I tried to return the man's intermittent stares; in the attempt
I noticed something utterly untoward and startling in his
expression.

The barbarian's mouth reminded me of Bronwen Lief's.
The dead girl shared with this archipelago dweller an almost
imperceptible pout, a downtugging of one corner of the
lower lip, that flawed an otherwise innocent and lovely face.

For the Pelagan was handsome. Despite the epicanthic
fold, despite the darkness of his complexion, despite the hair
on hands, arms, and face, he was imposingly handsome—in
a ruggedly exotic way that no Ongladredan ever could be.
But the set of his mouth! The set of his mouth sabotaged this
alien handsomeness. That he should share such a flaw with
Bronwen Lief, who had danced and declaimed as Gabriel
Elk had programmed her to, amazed me. In the upland cold,
the wind moaning through the rocks, I stared at him.

Then his eyes caught mine, and I had to look away.

Gareth was finished with him. "Are you going to take him back to Lunn in the coach?" the boy asked. He pulled the captive to his feet.

"No," Blaine said. "We have a dead man there already. The widow will ride with us, but I don't want Our Shathra Anna exposed to the Pelagan's presence any longer than is necessary; if possible, not at all. Ingram," turning to me, "I'd like you, young Elk here, and the ostler to walk the prisoner back to Lunn, if you would. We have no horses now but those on the carriage, and this man is too insolently disposed against us to bleed to death from his wounds on the trip back. I'm sorry to ask it, but I don't see any other immediate alternatives."

"Very well," I said. I didn't relish the walk, especially in the company of a man whose stare burned so piercingly.

Elk said, "You could leave the prisoner here tonight, Chancellor Blaine, and send someone back for him in the morning."

"No," Blaine said. "You may well have a secure place for him in Grotto House, but I want him back in Lunn as soon as possible. I intend to have him questioned quite thoroughly about the activities of Pelagan reivers and the likelihood of a concerted invasion by the entire Angromain. When? Where? How? I don't want there to be any chance at all that he might escape from your custody, Sayati Elk; the responsibility is too great."

"I'm not sure I want Gareth and Coigns on the Mershead Road tonight," the old man said. "They've been conscripted, yes, but their service doesn't begin until the day after tomorrow. Why should I let them go? A night is a long time, and it may be an even longer time after Gareth enters the Lunn garrison before Bethel and I see him again."

Blaine protested, "Ingram can't take this man back alone!"

"No," Gabriel Elk said. "The responsibility's too great. I don't propose that Master Marley go alone."

Arngrim Blaine pulled his cloak tight over his throat, crushing the lace there. His lips parted slightly; the carnelian tooth gleamed in the opening. He sensed some Elkian maneuver he would be powerless to avert. "Please, Sayati Elk, don't toy with me tonight. What is it you want?"

"Isn't it true you intend to cut short Master Marley's scrutiny of me and Stonelore? You're returning him to the palace?"

"That was my intention."

"I want him to stay."

"It was my impression you considered him a barely tolerable nuisance, Sayati Elk. He's been out here thirteen days eating your food, sleeping in your beds, an acknowledged agent of Our Shathra's Eyes and Ears—and tonight you decide you want him to stay? Why? Please enlighten me."

"The why is immaterial, Chancellor Blaine. My proposal is that I allow Gareth and Coigns to accompany Ingram and the prisoner *if* you send Ingram back to Stonelore on the day my son and the ostler report for duty—if not before."

"For how long?"

"Until Gareth and Coigns return."

Blaine looked at me with contempt. "You want to keep this indolent dirt-runner until the Halcyon Panic breaks, the Pelagans invade, the sloak crawls up, and Ongladred sinks into the Nathlin Trench? He's been on an extended sabbatical already, Sayati Elk, idling, idling every minute."

"I'll have work for him. Don't fear otherwise."

And so it was decided.

Our Shathra Anna and Rhia Lief climbed into the equipage with Arngrim Blaine, and the coachman galloped the tired horses through the Stonelore arena and down to the Mershead Road. Since there was no help for it, they went

unguarded—although both the coachman and the Chancellor
carried rifles on their laps.

As soon as they were gone, Gareth, Coigns, and I set off
with our Pelagan captive, whose renewed curses required us
to gag him again. Blood had welled up through the bandage
on his shoulder, but the man seemed none the worse for it.
"See that he's treated humanely, Ingram," Bethel Elk said to
me as we were leaving.

"Aye," her husband echoed her. "See to it."

Down from the upland arena we went on stiff legs. Wind
rippled the tall grasses. The Shattered Moons passed their
shadows through the wind and careened among themselves
like drunken soldiers. We reached Lunn well before dawn.
Robin Coigns and Gareth Elk returned at once to Stonelore,
refusing beds and breakfast at the Atarite Palace. I refused
only breakfast. I slept a long time, untroubled by any night-
mares of the murder I had committed.

Later, I learned that representatives of the Magi had tor-
tured the Pelagan captive for information. The man died on
the second day after our trek back from Stonelore; he died
without imparting a single nugget of intelligence—not his
name, not his dead companion's name, not the Angromain
island from which they had set out, not the purpose of their
reiving. Not anything. Every torture he had endured, revil-
ing his tormentors each time he could summon breath to do
so. A remarkable performance, the representatives of the
Magi said. I had slept through a good part of it, oblivious to
his suffering. What would the Elks say to me when I
returned?

Several days after the man's death, when I had firmly renewed my residence in Grotto House, three fishermen found
a two-man boat nine kilometers north of Mershead. The boat
had been concealed in a cave on the shoreline cliff faces; undoubtedly it had belonged to the men who had attacked us,

killed our horses, and murdered Josu Lief and the chariot guards. A two-man reiving party. Together they had come at least thirty kilometers, mostly at night, in an open boat.

On the side of the boat, painted there in a thick indigo pigment, was a cryptic symbol. It looked like this:

x

Gabriel Elk indeed had work for me. The state had taken Gareth away from him, and the spring equinox drew inexorably nearer. With the equinox's approach came also the beginning of the old man's annual series of neuro-dramas. In preparation for these, he forced me to undertake a strenuous apprenticeship. I was to serve as Gareth's replacement in the comptroller room beneath the Stonelore amphitheatre. That I had little aptitude for such work Gabriel Elk refused to concede. He had need of me.

So long as no more than three reanimated maskers were taking part in the action in the neuro-pit, the old man required no help. But when more actors moved into the sunken "stage" from below, another comptroller had to assist him. I was to be the second comptroller. During the concentrated weeks of my training, the old man permitted me very little time to myself. I learned everything about neuro-drama that Elk could impart and that I was capable of absorbing.

I learned that none of Gabriel Elk's compositions called for more than six performers. When operating with a full cast, he controlled three corpses and I controlled three. Neural programming prior to each performance took care only of facial expressions and speech; the majority of the actors' movements Elk and I had to direct from beneath the neuro-pit by remote control. Stamina was required of us because each drama adhered to rigid Aristotelian standards of unity, and we sometimes held our swivel chairs—amid console banks, sweat-inducing light, and closed-circuit television screens—for more than two hours at a stretch. An additional burden devolved upon us because the plays also invariably made use of pantomimic elements from an Oriental form called the *Noh* drama; these posings and gestures demanded of us a kind of agonizing, empathic monitoring. Moreover, we had to take care of Stonelore's lighting, the operation of the pneumatic lift in the center of the working area, and the synchronization of musical scores with the action going on overhead.

One of my most vivid memories of that time is of my introduction to the dead actors; this occurred on the second day after my return to Grotto House, when I was beginning my apprenticeship.

"Come, Ingram," Gabriel Elk said. "It's time you lost your innocence. We can't really begin work until you've seen them."

Together we went by elevator from the main level of Grotto House down into the programming room. Into the rock, into the realm of cybernetic miracles. But we didn't stop here. Elk guided me through this first crowded vault to a massive door opening on the tunnel leading to the Stone-lore comptroller room.

The tunnel, the entire underground complex, called up in me uncomfortable sensations of *déjà vu*—and not because I had once carried Bronwen Lief into the programming room; no, I felt as if in some indefinable past incarnation I had denied the light and entered a secret, subterranean mausoleum resembling this one, out of which I had emerged as pale as a dead man. The tunnel was lit by red lights; we stood for a moment in its mouth, looking toward the sealed comptroller room. Then we walked a few meters to a door on the corridor's righthand wall; here the old man admitted us to the dormitory of our dead colleagues, cohorts in Gabriel Elk's singular repertoire company.

This room was cold, icily cold.

The corpses that Elk had purchased lay in hard white plastic coffins, or preservators, with crystalline lids. A rank of three preservators on each side of the room, a narrow aisle in between. Each unit had its own self-regulating cryostat; all shared linkage with a central system of storage tanks containing liquid oxygen, these ice-touched canisters ranged like bright, upended cannon barrels against the far wall. Or like organ pipes.

Yes, I thought, *like organ pipes*. As if each sleeping actor were listening to cathedral music in the numb privacy of his own death, forevermore plugged into the storage tanks' silent anthems, the seethe of unendurable cold.

I looked down through the unfrosted glass of a preservator at Bronwen Lief's face. Unchanged, she slept.

I moved down the aisle.

Through the crystalline lids I looked at the faces of four men and another woman. The masker woman appeared haggish and diseased. The men offered almost a cross-section of the male Mansuecerian population, two being relatively young, one stout and middle-aged, the fourth cruelly wizened by six or seven decades of Ongladredan winters. These were Gabriel's players.

I looked back at my host. He began telling me the names of the five performers new to me. About each he recited a litany of biographical information: birthplaces, families, occupations, accomplishments, failures, and, finally, manners of dying.

"Did you know any of them while they were alive?" I asked him.

"No." He looked at me, then exhaled another puff of breath. "But I found out as much as I could about them over the winter. I bought all of them this past winter—except for Bronwen. I had to wait for her."

"You buy every winter?"

"I have to. I burn them out, Ingram. One season at Stonelore burns them out, as life never really has the chance to do."

"Do you program every one of them before the season begins? Then re-program them before each new play?"

"The ones who have roles always require surgical adaptation, electrode implanting, cybernetic neural grafting—the last of which enables us to control our performers from beneath the amphitheatre, Ingram. I'll work extensively on the ones who carry the brunt of the dramatic situation, less thoroughly on the others. Sometimes a performer will be masked, easing the preparatory burden on me; sometimes an actor or two will not have a speaking part. But the work's there, it exists. Your own efforts at Stonelore, Ingram, will be confined to the mechanics of immediate control, as were Gareth's; I'm not even going to try to introduce you to the other. That's my specialty, my hands and mind are inured to its tediousness."

"And when the season's over, Sayati Elk? What have you gained? And our burnt-out company of players," sweeping my arm backward over the sleek, insidiously still coffins, "what becomes of them?"

"Cremation. The funeral of Atarites rather than Mansuecerians, since in their last days—their artificial, posthumous lives—they will have behaved like people touched with fire. A death they have—then a brief, violently intense second life here at Stonelore—then a second, incontrovertible death. After which we put their burnt-out bodies to the torch and let the smoke curl up to Maz from the autumn bonfires."

I thought of the sloak, of the fires burning on every beach, inlet, and strip of coast around Ongladred. What must those tiny pyres look like from the air? If the Parfects were indeed orbiting our planet amid the concealing Shattered Moons, wouldn't they realize the bonfires were cries for help?

Standing in Elk's cryogenic locker, I shivered and shook the thought away. "But you, Sayati Elk," I said, returning to an old question, "what do you gain?"

His pale green eyes, combining ice and fire, lifted to mine; then he turned and walked out of the chamber, forcing me to follow.

Materially he gained very little.

On the nights when Elk and I sat in our cramped control niches beneath Stonelore, the Mansuecerians who filed into the theatre and filled its concentric tiers always "paid" for their seats, not so much from economic obligation as out of a ritualistic impulse to honor the old man. No one was forced to give anything, but nearly every masker made a token donation of three or four mithras when he entered, dropping the small coins into an open-mouthed urn beside the theatre's inner doors. Elk fed this money back to the state, which taxed him mercilessly. Or else, in the autumn and winter, he used the small surpluses remaining to him to buy new performers and to acquire materials unavailable to most Ongladredans. Genius and madman, he was neither fish nor fowl, masker nor Atarite; he bridged the social order.

He bought materials and equipment from Atarites whose wealth, station, and access to the Old Knowledge had bestowed upon them the benefits of an incipient technology. In fact, throughout his life Gabriel Elk had striven to assemble as many pieces of the Old Knowledge as he could buy, extort, or cajole from those privileged enough to possess it. His library in Grotto House was a tribute to this effort: forty thousand microchips, meticulously catalogued, all of them facsimiles of those the Parfects had given to humankind when we were dropped off, like so many unwanted curs, onto the rocky, gong-tormented planet of Mansueceria. Twice the Old Knowledge had survived the dissolution of Ongladredan civilization; twice it had been at least partially restored by foresighted men who had found one another in the ruins. Now Gabriel Elk had his share of it, and the neuro-dramas, I discovered, both drew upon the Old Knowledge and radically augmented it, made it new. So perhaps this was one of the things Gabriel Elk gained from Stonelore, the satisfaction of an omnivorous mind communing across time and interstellar distance with its intellectual forebears. But that wasn't the whole of it. After all, the process had begun with Elk long before Stonelore, and it would have gone on until the old man's death, in different manifestations, even if the amphitheatre had never been built.

Why, then, this kind of agonizing labor, the reanimating of corpses, the sweat and the emotional stridency of control? I didn't really have an answer.

One night, during the first week of the dramas, while Elk— helmeted and wired—was directing the action in the neuro- pit, I leaned back in my swivel chair and stared with bleary eyes at my console's central television screen.

There the haggish old woman and the middle-aged man acted out their parts in Elk's drama *Agon*. Life-sized figures projected as electrons through a cathode-ray tube and reassembled on the sensitized face of my receiver as tiny parodies of themselves. They hitched and spasmed on the screen,

seemingly kilometers away, even of another universe; thin
and metallic, almost garbled, their voices came through my
headset. The spectacle grew violent as the woman brand-
ished a temple knife and shrilly cursed her adversary.

How was our audience reacting?

I had no controlling to do for at least another fifty or sixty
lines. I turned in my chair. I saw Elk across the room from
me, his shoulders pushing forward, his arms stretched like
knotted cables over the console top, his fingers curled beneath eight different switches at once and ceaselessly shift-
ing among these. The cord-trailing helmet he wore gave him
the look of a stocky, bellicose medusa.

Facing my own console again, I directed one of the cam-
eras in the amphitheatre to scan our audience. I watched the
lefthand monitor above my comptroller unit. In Stonelore's
darkness the camera scanned by means of infrared floodlight-
ing and a quartz-lens relay. Tier after tier of masker faces, all
rigid beneath the movement of the camera, and because of
the ongoing conscription program many of these faces belonged to women, the elderly, and the very young.

I halted the camera. I brought a section of the audience
into startling close-up.

On my flickering monitor I studied the expressions on their
faces. A revelation discouragingly grim, not because the
maskers appeared either stern or disapproving but because
their eyes and mouths betrayed no emotion at all; they sat,
merely sat, gazing down upon our actors and partaking of
Elk's surcharged dramaturgy as if it were no more real than
an indifferent daydream.

Faces rigid with blandness; eyes too wide-awake and at-
tentive to suggest apathy, but so noncommittal as to be
damn-near inhuman.

As I watched the faces on the monitor, I began to feel that
our audience wanted reanimating even more than had our

dead actors, the ones who now vigorously shadowed forth Gabriel Elk's vision. The dead vicariously living through the dead, our audience seemed.

Then I had to go to work again. My visor came down. The pneumatic lift carried another actor into the arena, this one a young man under my direction. My eyes turned from the lefthand monitor to the screen in the center. Watching this, I let my hands direct the movements of my protégé's hands; I wandered into his mind, then activated Elk's neural programming of the speech centers, and withdrew. My presence was external then, a transferral of will conveyed by delicate mechanical means and the aching implementation of rote memory—mine. For twenty more minutes I sweated (eventually controlling Bronwen Lief as well as the young masker) while Elk deployed every one of his corpses and kept them all hitching and spasming about like the decrepit primitives they were supposed to be: a *tour de force* of comptrolling.

Then *Agon* was over.

Wearily I leaned back in my chair. I looked at my lefthand monitor and saw that the closed-circuit camera was still scanning our audience, relaying their images into the comptroller room as they sat unmoving and seemingly unmoved in the rising houselights. Again, that infuriating and universal expressionlessness!

Finally they stood and, talking desultorily with one another or saying nothing at all, filed out of Stonelore into the night, a regiment of automatons. When they were gone, the amphitheatre was no more quiet than it had been while they were there. I turned to Elk, who had unhelmeted himself and swiveled toward me.

"Three nights in a row, Sayati Elk. Are they always like that?"

"Yes. Usually." His sideburns were matted, the lower portions curled moistly over his cheeks; his eyes red-rimmed and narrow. He looked very old that night, every one of his sixty-three years.

"You mean we can expect a response no more lively than what we've had these last three nights?"

ı "Probably not a bit livelier than this, Ingram."

"A regiment of automatons," I said. "Blaine's conscripted almost all the men of fighting age, but there's still a regiment of automatons—several regiments—in Lunn, Brechtlin, and Mershead; they come out to Stonelore every night."

"Different ones come on different nights, Ingram. And they're not, as you would style them, *automatons.*"

"How judge a masker except on the basis of his behavior, Sayati Elk?"

"With the People Accustomed to the Hand one has to judge on the basis of *significant,* not just conspicuous, behavior."

I shook my head. "I don't understand you, Sayati Elk; I've sweated through this with you three times now and still don't understand why you do it. The money is nothing to you, and the maskers file out every evening as if they've simply wanted a warm place to sit for an hour or two. It demoralizes me, Sayati Elk, it guts me of purpose and initiative. Whereas you . . ." My unfinished sentence hung in the room between the two of us.

Then Elk said, "Whereas I notice that they come back, Ingram. No one forces them to come, but they come back— performance after performance in the spring and summer, year after year."

He stood up. "They always come back," he reiterated quietly.

Then we went about the task of securing the comptroller room and caring for our feverish performers. I worked without speaking, in a spirit of weary half-comprehension of what he had told me and of listless ignorance of what he had left out. We spent a good deal of time pushing the mobile pre-servators up and down the tunnel.

Afterwards I slept, slept dreamlessly. And woke on the next morning to anticipate another evening in the comptrol-ler room—for, as usual, Stonelore would be full.

xi

Away from Stonelore things were happening. During the fifteen successive presentations of *Agon* events in the outside world threatened to break in upon us, to force us out of our isolation.

The far northern coasts of Ongladred, four hundred kilometers from Lunn, had begun to suffer the first of a number of Pelagan naval assaults. From what we heard, these were not merely the hit-and-run tactics of foolhardy reivers operating singly and apparently at whim, but the tentative strikes of a nation testing its full-scale capacities for war. Usually one or two large Pelagan vessels slipped through the veils of night and wind-whipped spray to fire their cannons at a coastal village and the small ships in harbor there. The bonfires crackling jewel-like at intervals along the coast to hold off the sloak did nothing but illuminate the barbarians' targets, betray the simple people who had set the fires.

Prows like dragons, sails like reptilian wings, banners like streaming serpents' tongues, witnesses said. Then, having wrought their sudden destruction, the ships were gone back into the night and the mocking sea wind.

But the little fishing village of Nogos, we heard, had not escaped so easily; the Pelagans had come ashore, murdered most of the citizenry in their beds, abducted perhaps twenty more people, and then fled seaward. The following day several fishermen from south of Nogos found bodies floating in their fishing grounds; most of the corpses had been stricken at and mutilated by boarnoses (sharklike creatures infesting the iciest waters of the Angromain Run). On the second morning after the attack at Nogos, two or three more bodies were washed up by the tide near Thumbre.

Because of the latitude and their remove from the main islands of the Angromain Archipelago, the people in the north of Ongladred had felt themselves safe from this kind of brutal harassment. The Atarite Court in Lunn had agreed; most of the state's forces were positioned along our island's southern and eastern coasts, and not only because Arngrim Blaine wished to preserve Lunn over any other Ongladredan city. No. Lunn was vulnerable, that was all. The greatest portion of our navy, therefore, lay just off the coasts where our troops were encamped, a defensive barrier against the Pelagan fleet. Reivers had penetrated the barrier at night, yes, but Blaine reasoned that our enemies would have a difficult time sneaking a hundred large warships past us. Now it appeared that the Pelagans would not even try; instead they would sail their dragon vessels east from their own islands, away from Ongladred, circle then toward the polar cap, and descend on us from the White Sea and the multicolored Angromain Run.

Two days after the devastation of Nogos, four after the first hit-and-run raids on other villages, Our Shathra Anna ordered a reprisal.

She ordered seven of our galleons to strike swiftly and heavily at Orcland, the largest island of the Angromain group and the suspected seat of the newly centralized Pelagan government.

At Stonelore, Elk and I were preparing for the ninth performance of *Agon*. We were in complete ignorance of what was happening over seventy kilometers out to sea. Later we learned.

The reprisal strike had failed.

Several ships of the Pelagan fleet had intercepted our galleons more than an hour from the Orcland coast. Firing without warning, they had sunk three Ongladredan raiders, captured one ship, crippled two more, and sent the cripples limping home in the wake of our only unscathed galleon. Our enemies, it seemed, were strong, resourceful, and determined to establish themselves, eventually, as masters of Ongladred.

That much we learned; little more.

For the most part, Gabriel Elk ignored these developments, although on two or three occasions I managed to draw him into brief, unrevealing discussions. The only link he and Bethel recognized between themselves and the fortunes of the state was their son, Gareth. He and Coigns had been assigned away from the Lunn garrison to the infantry forces of Pavan Nils Barrow, now encamped outside the northern coastal city of Thumbre. Bethel Elk, from all external appearances, saw this link as much more significant than her husband did; she feared for her son, but she also feared for Field-Pavan Barrow and the people of Firthshir Province.

One day she asked me, "Do you think the Pelagans will

land up there, Ingram?" She faced me stiffly, her back held erect by the brace.

"I don't know. Except for a few reivers, they've shown a general reluctance to put us to the trial down here—if that tells us anything. The raids on Nogos and the other villages must mean something, too, Mistress Elk. A clue to their plans."

"It's almost summer now," she said. "But it's still cold up there, isn't it, Ingram? Like winter?"

"Yes. Or very early spring."

"Gareth and Coigns have blankets and woolen coats. I hope the others are as lucky." Then she left me where I sat, in Grotto House's open courtyard, enjoying the warmth of pale Maz.

During the days, Gabriel Elk left me to myself.

He spent most of his time reworking the formal lyric passages of the dramas he had composed over the winter. A little time he spent in the programming room, forecasting the methods and the equipment he would use in preparing our actors for new roles. As soon as *Agon* was over, the mechanical work would begin. In the interval he concentrated on perfecting the odes and the rhymed variety of stichomythia in which he often had his characters speak, parrying epigram with epigram. All I could get from him was that the next two dramas completed a trilogy whose subject was "human suffering and achievement." After which pronouncement, he grinned.

First, *Agon*. Then plays entitled *Anabasis in Spring* and *Omega Thwarted*. The titles meant nothing to me, but Elk gave me to understand that the trilogy represented a new direction in his work. Again, I didn't know. I had neither seen nor read any of his previous neuro-dramas.

Now he was revising *Anabasis in Spring*. I had nothing to do but wander about Grotto House thinking on the frivolity of "enlightening" the masker population of Lunn, Brechtlin, and Mershead while the villages of Firthshir Province burned. An enlightened masker, as far as I could see, behaved no differently from one who dwelt in deadpan ignorance.

Then our fifteen performances of *Agon* were over. The island was growing into summer—real summer—with meadow flowers nodding yellow and blue heads among the dull upland grasses. Fifteen days we had; then Elk and I would be back in the rending, grey world of the comptroller room.

Our fifteen days out of the comptroller room were no vacation. Although we did get to see the anaita-roses fluttering—and the little blue flowers whose name I never learned (but remembered from Rhia Lief's embroidery)—and to feel the southerly sea wind, the *maloob*, blow like invisible velvet over our skins, these respites were rare. While Elk prepared corpses, I prepared myself. That preparation consisted of reading *Anabasis in Spring* and studying as well its diagram-laden companion, a Manual of Control. This last was a bleak little booklet in Elk's own minute longhand. Like some of the flowers around Stonelore, the ink (I remember) was violet.

As summer came on, so did the rumor and the fact of Pelagan hostility. On one of these days between dramas, during the period of preparation, I caught Elk in Grotto House's dining chamber and sat down beside him. "I'm afraid I'm beginning to be of Chancellor Blaine's persuasion, Sayati Elk. What we're doing, how do we justify it? I can appreciate the aesthetic experience of the neuro-dramas, or at least I can before the tedium of comptrolling blunts my responses—but too many things are happening beyond Stonelore, things of genuine moment, for me to rest easy here any longer. I'd like to go back to Lunn, to the Atarite Palace."

"Oh?" The old man leaned back in his chair, a heavy

wooden chair with thick arms. "What will you do when you get back there, volunteer for a seaman's position?"

"As a member of the court, even as a relatively obscure dirt-runner, I'm—"

"You're exempt from any such demeaning service. I know, Ingram. So what will you do while 'things of genuine moment' confront your countrymen?"

"Whatever Our Shathra Anna and Chancellor Blaine require of me."

"Ah, duty; a noble sentiment, Master Marley." It had been a while since he had slapped me with "Master Marley." "For now, because Gareth's been taken from me, they require you to serve Ongladred by aiding me."

"The two are equivalent, I suppose?"

"No, no, Ingram. I don't suffer from that delusion. Besides, as you know, Arngrim Blaine doesn't equate the two. To keep you out here, I intimidated him."

"Then we're back to my original question, Sayati Elk. If my service to you isn't really service to Ongladred, why do we nearly kill ourselves for an audience whose only response is to come back as listless as they left? What are we accomplishing?" I had to pin the old man down.

But he said, "Service is of different types, Ingram, and some varieties of it lie outside the stagnant pale of nationalism and duty. This is one of those. What we're accomplishing, though, I won't try to tell you—won't even try to articulate yet for myself. I'm a selfish old man, Ingram. *Selfish* and *old,* those are the key words. And if I'm deluded at all, it may be in the assumption that my selfishness serves Ongladred better than would a dutiful renunciation of self. At least for now. This, like all things, may change. . . ."

And so we ignored the continuing depredations in the north; we forgot the fragrance of the anaita-roses, the freshness of the maloob blowing inland across a summer ocean.

Here is a summary of that time: The Ongladredan fleet overextended itself attempting to establish a defensive line across the coasts of Firthshir, Vestacs, and Eenlich provinces; Elk and I, toward the end of our fifteen-day preparation period, began giving up great chunks of sleep time, courting exhaustion. Galleons burned; my morale sank. Rumors of impending invasion reached us via the itinerant tinkers and tradesboys who sometimes stopped at Grotto House; in my sleep I saw the amphitheatre filling with maskers who wore under faces bitingly vacant, tunics emblazoned with this: Then, receiving only token resistance, the Pelagans landed an army of almost eight thousand men in Eenlich; on the evening of that day Gabriel Elk opened Stonelore for the first performance of *Anabasis in Spring*. Just as the Angromain barbarians had committed themselves in the north, we too had gone past the point of abjuration. Two darkly improbable enterprises had been set in motion, the Pelagans' and ours.

"How do you like the title of my play now?" Gabriel Elk asked me. "I'm a prophet in my own land, unhonored and indifferent to my neglect. The Pelagans, your erstwhile brothers, Atarites under the skin, march upon us. And my play predicts it."

"Pillars crumble. People die. And we—"

"—*fiddle*. Is that the word you're looking for? Remember one thing, Ingram: Gareth's up there in Firthshir, with Barrow's forces."

I turned away from him. So he was aware, coldly aware of the situation. Why, then, our singlemindedness in putting on a neuro-drama, in running corpses through an intricate, *unreal* series of events? Apparently Elk had his own satisfactions; I had only the sweat. My back to Gabriel Elk, I looked at the lefthand monitor.

Our audience was filing in.

"People die," the old man was saying, talking to the back of my head. "But not these. These still live, Ingram." I could feel his eyes fixed on my monitor. Together we watched the audience come in:

Women, children, old men, cripples of every conceivable sort:

The bent, the legless, the scarred, the humpbacked, even the blind. All of them People Accustomed to the Hand, maskers who had come to Stonelore for undivulged reasons of their own.

Then Elk swiveled away from me, faced his own control console, signaled to me that we were about to begin. I put on my helmet, shut out my thoughts, turned a dial, and plunged the amphitheatre into darkness. The sweat, the sweat of comptrolling.

And that night Elk and I, working together, working begrudgingly together, orchestrated a beautiful performance of *Anabasis in Spring*. The poetry came through my headset; the alternating grace and clumsiness of our actors poured into me like haoma. I was a part of Elk's poetry, I was a part of our actors' movement. The sweat of comptrolling turned into the sweat of participation.

In the neuro-pit above us two dead men are discussing the cycle of the sloak; I am both dead men, two young soldiers. Then enter the corpse of the haggish old woman, inhabited now by Gabriel Elk. She is masked like a demon, somehow enormous and dreadful in spite of her tiny bones and frail gestures. To the soldiers she is an apparition, a minion of hidden powers. In a long, image-crowded speech she tells them the sloak is real, that it does the bidding not of its own protoplasmic desires but of a watchful intelligence external to itself—an intelligence vastly more alive than Man's but different in kind. She dances while she speaks, and her huge, one-eyed mask seems to float between her upraised arms like a kite to which her thin, twisting body is the knotted tail. As the accompaniment of tabor and flute grows more insistent, her head—her leering mask—threatens to pull her aloft, lift her into soaring flight. But the music stops, her speech ends, and the hag disappears into the underworld. The two soldiers whom I inhabit stare after her in awe and consternation.

That scene, even in the observation of *Elk's* comptrolling, wrung me of energy. There were other such scenes.

Anabasis in Spring dealt not only with the threat of the sloak, but also with the problems of command in an army relentlessly on the march. It was not prophecy, as Elk had said it was, because one could not help feeling that the sloak and the army in this neuro-drama existed in an altogether different realm of experience, another world; everything was distanced, set at a remove—in spite of which the actions and feelings of the characters had an uncanny immediacy.

Still, though overwhelmed by the poetry and the detail Elk had lavished on this spectacle, I knew that it wasn't real. What relation did it have to reality? To the sloak and to the Pelagan forces? The real sloak, the real invaders? So absolutely powerful in Stonelore's comptroller room, Elk and I were ironically powerless in the face of these threatening certainties. Was Elk withdrawing into prophecy, abandoning the real for the sake of artificial order and contrived significance? He had said no. He had said that I ought to remember the dilemma of his son, which he had not forgotten either—which he could not forget.

Wrung out at play's end, I pushed my visor back and remembered nothing, thought nothing. The sweat of comptrolling, the sweat of participation, was dry on my neck. Elk stood behind me, a hand on my shoulder. Together we watched the maskers file out: the women, the children, the old men, the crippled and the deformed. Their faces were as dull as the underside of a leaf, their eyes were the wicks of guttered candles. Only a few of them talked.

"Nothing," I said. "Nothing."

We presented *Anabasis in Spring* on three more evenings. Then stopped—but not because of this lack of discernible response on our audience's part. No. Events intervened, events and Our Shathra Anna. Against history and royalty Gabriel Elk ultimately had no more resources than did the simplest masker. And on the following morning history and royalty came to Grotto House in the person of Chancellor Arngrim Blaine.

PART TWO

xii

His roan tooth glistening, slashing like a miniature tusk, Arngrim Blaine said, "The Halcyon Panic has broken, Sayati Elk. It's broken, and I believe your neuro-dramas have been instrumental in destroying our citizenry's calm." Anger lay under the planes of his thin, expressive face like a ripening bruise.

"Obviously you haven't attended a neuro-drama this season," I said. We were sitting in Gabriel Elk's quiet little study on the main level of Grotto House; the room contained leatherbound books—not microchips, but books. Both the Elks were present, in adjacent, meticulously carven chairs.

Bethel said, "The people have been kept abreast of the events in Firthshir, haven't they?"

"They have, Mistress Elk."

89

"Then how can you blame the people's distress—the breaking of the panic, as you call it, Chancellor—on my husband's dramas, not a one of which you have seen in its entirety? The Lief girl's performance doesn't count."

"I can do so, Mistress Elk, because things have culminated much too soon; the misdirected rage the young women of Lunn have exhibited in the last two days comes well ahead of schedule, it defies the computations of the Magi."

Gabriel Elk said, "But then again, Chancellor Blaine, the Pelagan invasion has taken place sooner than the Magi expected."

"And the rage of the young Mansuecerian women, the wives of our soldiers and seamen," Bethel Elk said, "has been growing for a long time. That rage has been building since well before the Magi decreed the existence of a 'Halcyon Panic.' It's the product of a long-ingrained and periodically aggravated sense of helplessness, which I feel too, Chancellor Blaine."

"I don't doubt that you do. However, Our Shathra Anna—who is, as I shouldn't have to remind you, a woman too—says that the 'sense of helplessness' you speak of need not reveal itself in hysteria and acts of vandalism."

Bethel Elk said, "Our Shathra Anna's experience has hardly been typical."

A chill descended upon Gabriel Elk's study, like a dust of invisible snow sifting out of the very air. We were all as separate as corpses put up in our own sealed, sound-muffling preservators. Who would resurrect us?

I looked at Blaine, sitting cross-legged opposite me. He had come to Grotto House that morning dressed not as the Chancellor of Ongladred, nor even as a member of the Atarite Court, but instead like a reasonably successful masker trades-man. Two young guards had accompanied him, posing as his sons. All these precautions had grown out of the wish to prevent a visit as disastrous as Our Shathra Anna's last one. And yet the Chancellor had come himself, he had not sent a representative.

Coolly he said, "Listen to me. Two days ago—the day after your newest production had opened, Sayati Elk—a large group of young women left Lunn, marched out the Mershead Road, and began turning over vegetable booths and fish stalls. Not the ones run by old men or other women, but those tended by masker tradesmen whom we've exempted from military service—or else booths owned by minor Atarite officials. There was no stopping these women."

"In that case," Gabriel Elk laughed, "your choice of disguises could have been wiser."

Arngrim Blaine ignored this. "That night a pack of children—turned loose by their mothers, I've no doubt—ran into the thoroughfare beneath my offices and began chanting a litany to Maz, asking Him to blow Himself up and Ongladred, too, so that we might at least die in the light." The Chancellor permitted himself a wan smile. "We had no success either in catching the children or in driving them away; the ones whom the guards did catch were inevitably replaced by others, all crying together, 'Maz, Maz, destroy us in light. Preserve us from the slime of the sloak and the knives of barbarians. Let the lie die.' A litany drummed into them by women."

"Your sleep was spoiled," Bethel Elk commiserated.

"Oh, that episode has its amusing aspects; I'm not blind to them. But that same night some hysterical person, or group of persons, set fire to a row of dwellings on Lunn's southwestern outskirts. The houses all burned, and several people died, including children, Mistress Elk. A violet pall of smoke hung over the rooftops, quite lurid under the Shattered Moons, I assure you. And yesterday the wail of keening women filled the streets—issued from every house—from dawn until long after nightfall, a general lamentation the likes of which I've never heard in Lunn. I'm surprised you didn't hear it out here.

"Then yesterday—since the keening doesn't by any means end the matter—a procession of old women, as many as two hundred or so, walked all the way from Lunn to Brechtlin, on the point opposite Mershead, and disrobed on the beaches. After that, they waded into the sea and kept wading until their strength gave out and they drowned. These were widows, unmarried women, grandmothers. None of the Mansuecerian population tried to stop them; that they be left alone seemed to be the unspoken desire of even their relatives. We dispatched a few Atarite guardsmen to turn them back, but the women wouldn't be reasoned with—and simple coercion failed, from want of enough men to restrain them. Into the water they went, naked pathetic creatures obeying an hysteria beyond my comprehension, Mistress Elk. Even now they are being buried, all the washed-ashore corpses no one will come forward to identify.

"And these things—the arson, the keening, the senseless suicides—are *not* amusing, friends. They betoken the depth of our citizenry's fear."

A different kind of silence filled the study then. Arngrim Blaine had reasserted his dignity. The four of us sat there, self-conscious, in its palpable aura. At last Bethel said, "And you believe that *Agon* and *Anabasis in Spring* are responsible for these things, Chancellor?"

"In part, yes."

"I would like to think you are right," the old man said.

"May I ask why?" the Chancellor said curtly.

"Certainly. Everyone requires a degree of power, no matter how minute."

"Of this sort? Power to cause suicides and arson?"

"If one is weak, yes. However, I'm not a weak man, Chancellor, and that's not what I require in power. I see in these atypical patterns of behavior—this hysteria—the potential for something constructive. It's that germ of constructiveness I would like to think my neuro-dramas help nourish. In all the negative acts of the last three days there is a thin, affirmative thread."

"Very thin." The Chancellor's lips hardly parted. "Very thin."

I said, "The best explanation for this behavior is not the neuro-dramas, but the news from Firthshir."

"That figures prominently," Chancellor Blaine said. "Certainly I don't dismiss it. In fact, I ought to tell you that the Pelagan forces have pushed out of Firthshir into Eenlich Province, driving Field-Pavan Barrow's army before them." He paused. "There's no word of casualties. As far as I know, Gareth and Coigns are alive. On this point I can't say any more; I don't know any more.

"Messages have described the retreats as 'strategic,' but the fact remains that we're losing ground daily. Fields are being burned, early crops destroyed, animals slaughtered, and small hamlets overrun and subsequently abandoned. The enemy supplies himself at our expense. This is changing, however. A runner from Pavan Barrow reports that our people have begun to destroy any goods that may be useful to the Pelagans; the procedure now is burn and fall back, burn and fall back. We want to force the barbarians to be dependent on their own supply lines—in the hope that we can establish an unmoving front and then interdict at sea, destroy their own naval logistics system. But their troops have been reinforced almost three times a week, and we now estimate an invading army of almost twenty thousand men. If they continue to advance at twelve to fifteen kilometers a day, they will reach Lunn before the month is out. Ongladred will fall."

"Why have you made a special trip to Stonelore to tell us

these things?" Bethel Elk asked. "Surely, Chancellor, you don't hold the neuro-dramas responsible for the Pelagan invasion?"

"No, not that, Mistress Elk." He turned to Gabriel. "Do you remember the conversation we had here at Grotto House after Bronwen Lief's recital, before the reivers murdered Josu Lief?"

"I remember it," the old man said. "You're not going to offer me the command of a Mansuecerian vessel again, are you?"

"No. That's not the portion of the conversation I'm referring to."

"Then which?"

"You and your son argued strongly that societies fail when their leaders fail. You cited inflexibility as the most dangerous sin of command. Do you remember?"

"I remember."

"And do you remember that Our Shathra Anna told you that one day you would have to include yourself among the number of Ongladred's leaders?"

"Yes, that too—more or less. Although I believe we made a distinction between intellectual and political leadership."

I almost laughed, but Chancellor Blaine was maneuvering craftily, as if born to the Socratic method; I watched him with genuine interest. Gabriel Elk, his large hands on his knees now, was also intrigued, a man ensnared in spite of himself.

"Distinctions such as that blur," the Chancellor was saying, "when the enemy plants his boots on our own soil, Sayati Elk. See me here before you," spreading his hands self-deprecatingly, "I am trying to bend. Our Shathra Anna bids me remind you that in these times we must all bend, particularly the leaders among us. If you feel that Ongladred is worth preserving, either for its own virtues or in preference to the barbaric code that would supplant our own, you too must bend, Sayati Elk. You must—"

"There will be no more performances at Stonelore this season, Chancellor. At least for a while."

Slowly Arngrim Blaine closed his mouth, cut off in mid-harangue. I, too, was surprised; the old man had said nothing to me about discontinuing the neuro-dramas. He had not even hinted at it. It was a course he had only just decided upon, it was his own preemptive strike—a means of regaining the initiative. And yet he struck out of belief, not out of wounded pride or insecurity; that his decision nonplused the Chancellor merely increased his cold, grey delight in affirming a conviction. Elk leaned back; his hands came off his knees.

"Good," Blaine said. "That was easier than I expected."

"I don't do it to please you," Gabriel Elk told him, "but because Ongladred is threatened and I am not a fool. I had hoped that Field-Pavan Barrow and our ships in the channel would save me a decision like this one, but that's past recall now—a dead hope. The news you've brought tonight, Chancellor, wounds and frightens me, me a man almost inured to pain and too old to get very frightened anymore. Therefore, Stonelore closes."

"But what else does the Chancellor wish?" Mistress Elk asked. "Will you place Gabriel in command of a galleon?"

"No. That would be too little, Mistress Elk, a misapplication of talents. Our Shathra wants something more."

"A weapon," Gabriel Elk said.

Again Arngrim Blaine looked surprised, almost incredulous. He uncrossed his legs and extended them straight out before him. "Yes," he said. "An unconventional weapon, something that can be developed in twenty days or less, easily transported, and deployed in the field."

The old man looked at the ceiling and laughed, a sardonic

yap. I started, so unexpected was this noise. Then Elk folded his hands in his lap and scrutinized them like a sculptor taking mental notes. "A weapon," he mused.

"That's principally why we want Stonelore closed," Blaine said, "so that you can devote your time to this project—although my own feeling is that secondary benefits will accrue, the foremost among these being the return to calm of Lunn's populace. Our Shathra Anna wishes you to begin at once. Will you?"

"Why don't you put your Atarite scientists to work on this, Chancellor? They have the Old Knowledge, the materials, the technological capacity—or at least its potential." Elk clasped his huge hands together. "Why do you trek out here to ask of me this pretty little enormity?"

"Oh, we have the technological capacity to do everything you have done, Sayati Elk. We also have the materials, the physical resources. It's the psychic capacity that we lack. Were it not for this inhibition, an inhibition programmed into us by the Parfects several thousand years ago, the People touched by Fire would have created self-propelled carriages, atomic-driven ships, mechanized communication systems, even vehicles that fly—all of these things we would have developed long ago. The knowledge is there, but we don't permit ourselves to use it; we are inhibited, *psychically* inhibited, and even our recognition of this fact doesn't cure us, Sayati Elk. In this case, self-awareness is not power. We have heated and lighted the Atarite palace, and a number of Atarite lords have done the same with the houses on their estates—but beyond that we haven't ventured, we haven't *wanted* to venture. What you have done at Stonelore and Grotto House doesn't confound our intellects, it confounds our sense of propriety, it mocks something innate and immovable in our natures. That's what we've come to you for, Sayati Elk. Those are our reasons. Do you understand?"

"Yes. I'm an aberration."

"That's a pejorative term I would not have used. Please don't try to attribute it to me. What I mean is that you are not inhibited in the way of either those Accustomed to the Hand or those Touched by Fire. Your aggressiveness is intellectual as well as physical."

I said, "You're Ongladred's superman, Sayati Elk, Zoroaster's übermensch."

Ignoring this, Elk said, "The Parfects re-created Man in a strange, divided image, Chancellor Blaine. They did not want us to kill ourselves, but they didn't want us to die, either. Mansuecerians. Atarites. A strange, divided people struggling together to subdue Ongladred. Then, a thousand years ago, we divided again, and what the Parfects tried to provide against is happening once more. We're killing one another, but even as we do we excuse ourselves on the grounds that it isn't yet genocide, the extinction of the species. Neither the Pelagans nor the ruling order in Ongladred has essayed a genocidal weapon; something in our shared unconscious will not allow the attempt. And yet today, Chancellor, you ask me to commit myself to the development of the first such horror on the road to just that end, the end of being able to destroy utterly, without mercy or discrimination."

"Because you have the skill," Blaine said. Then added killingly: "And the temperament."

"The temperament!" Bethel Elk said.

"Yes, Mistress Elk. The temperament that conceived and raised the miracle of Stonelore out of the dust of this upland arena."

"Oh come now, Chancellor. Your language apotheosizes my husband."

"Its intention, Mistress, is quite the opposite. It's because Sayati Elk is more 'human' than we," keeping his face composed, decorously humble, avoiding even the hint of smugness, "that we ask this of him."

"My difference from the members of the Atarite Court," Elk said, "is not so great that it frees me from the sanctions of our shared unconscious."

Arngrim Blaine sighed. Then he pulled his tradesman's clothes together, smoothed out the wrinkles in his breeches, and stood. "Very well. Then I'll tell Our Shathra Anna that although Stonelore is closing, you cannot bring yourself to do something no Atarite will attempt." I was impressed, then, by Blaine's fairness; he might have said something as self-servingly crass as "cannot bring yourself to *save* Ongladred," but he had not: Conscience had prevailed.

"Sit down," Elk said. "Tell Our Shathra Anna that in twenty days—with the help of those Atarite lords who can supply me with information and materials—I will give her what she wishes."

Blaine eased himself back in his chair. "You have the complete cooperation of the court, Sayati Elk."

"Then I must also have your promise to return the weapons to me when we have defeated the Pelagans. The weapons will be small and deadly—but in themselves they'll fall mercifully short of any sort of doomsday weapon. Still, I want your word that afterwards, after our victory, the weapons will come back to me—without fail."

"You have it, Sayati Elk."

"Good. Then let's stop talking and have something to drink. Ingram, will you serve us."

I said that I would; got up; went down the hall to the kitchen. I could not believe that the evening would not find Gabriel Elk and me helmeted, wired, and perspiring in our swivel chairs in the comptroller room. Before I returned to the study, I had a solitary drink of haoma and let several scenes of *Anabasis in Spring* play through my mind. I would never see them again, except in my mind. Somehow that struck me—for reasons I then refused to consider deeply—as a poignant loss.

And that evening we turned away a crowd of masker women, children, and old men, telling them the amphitheatre had been closed. Unprotesting, they went back through the upland grasses, down to the Mershead Road, and returned from whence they had come—to tell their friends the news.

xiii

The following day Gabriel Elk began work. He used the facilities in the programming room under Grotto House. Bethel handled the correspondence that the project required, writing letters in her small, looping hand and sealing them with purple wax and the impress of Chancellor Blaine's ring. I carried the letters. To the homes of the landed Atarites, to the offices of our scientists, I rode. Always I returned to Grotto House; and soon wagons of materials—chemicals, metals, precious stones, boxed unknowables—began rattling up into the dusty arena and leaving behind their cargoes. On several occasions men whom I didn't know arrived with stern or expressionless faces, disappeared into the programming room, remained a day or two, then emerged and departed, not to be seen at Grotto House again.

Ten days passed. I found myself thinking that if not for the Pelagan invasion, we would have just concluded our second neuro-drama and begun preparations for the third.

Omega Thwarted. Appropriate title, it seemed. I had not even read the play, had no idea what sort of end it would mark to Elk's trilogy or which corpses he had hoped would carry the burden of its theme; for the moment, they all lay inviolately frozen in their preservators, darkness and ice weaving about them a smoky, blue shroud. In dreams, I saw the faces of the corpses growing a fine, weblike covering of hair, their eyes simultaneously narrowing—until they all resembled the reivers who had attacked us so many nights ago. Then I woke to the nightmare in the north.

Field-Pavan Barrow's forces had begun to slow the Pelagan advance—but the countryside through which they retreated, burning what our own people had built or planted, stretched away to the White Sea like a desert of ash. So our runners said. Firthshir, Eenlich, and Vestacs provinces had been transmogrified into the Fields of Astivihad; they were diseased deathscapes in which charred tree trunks and unfilled graves lay desolate under a thin sun and no birds broke the silence with their songs. At sea, several more of our galleons had been sunk, and even in Lunn we could feel the breaths of an animalish people hot and rank on our faces. The enemy was only a little more than a hundred kilometers away, momentarily stalled. Or so our runners told us and so we hoped. . . .

The fighting continued. Even young Atarite men were being sent to the front (those who could command were already there), and I expected at any hour to hear my own summons. At times I wished for it, so futile and anticipatory did my own privileged role seem. What was Elk doing? Though I slept in his house, I seldom got the chance to talk to him. At the front, I imagined, there would be continuous conversation of a lethal kind, the bass imperatives of cannon and the high-pitched yawping of rifles. Old, damn-near falling-to-pieces Yorkley rifles.

What kind of advantage was Elk going to give us?

On the sixteenth day after Arngrim Blaine's second visit to Stonelore, two empty, closed wagons arrived at the arena. Gabriel Elk directing, we spent the late morning and all the afternoon carrying equipment out of the programming room to the wagons. Up and down in the elevator, back and forth through the stone corridor. I worked with four masker laborers, handicapped men who had not been inducted; I struggled to preserve my dignity before them, sometimes attempting to lift more than I was able. Not long past, hadn't I come from these people?

Elk and I rode horseback (on creatures provided by the Atarite Court, animals which Elk eventually bought outright) beside the wagons on our way to Lunn. At sunset we reached the Atarite Palace and drove through the cobbled court to the great, white-stone recreation building. Here we unloaded our materials, setting them up in the vast athletic hall exactly as Elk told us.

Once, as I passed him, the old man said, "Your fire-touched friends will have to forego their genteel pellet-ball and fencing for a day or two, Ingram."

The hall was fiercely illuminated, the electric flambeaux rippled with the energy coursing into them, and the palace (as far as I could judge, outside, from the evidence of its muted windows) was almost dark by comparison—as if the recreation hall were draining some of its power away. Before we had finished unloading, Arngrim Blaine himself came out of the palace and approached the recreation hall; he came with two of the men who had been to Grotto House during the early stages of Elk's work. For the first time, their faces wore looks of ill-concealed excitement.

The wagons rattled away. In the shadow between two great buildings, we five men conferred. Chancellor Blaine said, "Master Gordon and Sayati Snow have told me nothing about this enterprise, Sayati Elk, except that it progresses. Does it?"

"No further, I hope, than it has already."

"What have you developed?"

"A device I call a photon-director. And I have merely developed it, not created it. The Old Knowledge preserved for us by the Parfects contains an incomplete and deliberately cryptic 'description' of the instrument and an abstract of its theory, including a list of applications. The applications are all benevolent—from precision measurement to the healing of retinal lesions."

"Then . . . ?"

"Don't fear, Chancellor. I haven't been working these last sixteen days to manufacture a machine of mercy. The Parfects explicitly told us nothing, nothing at all, about how to murder one another by such a device. But the information's there for minds profound enough to dig it out." The old man spoke as if each word scalded him. "Profound enough," he reiterated. "And *flexible* enough. In times such as these flexibility is a cardinal virtue."

"And genius," the Chancellor said placatingly, sensitive to Elk's tone. And between Blaine's parted lips, the carnelian gleam of that tooth—a little tusk, a knife of discolored bone. And then the lips closed.

"Genius is a hag who flies in the heart," Elk said. "This was different, this was a toad squatting there."

"But it works?"

"It works. Master Gordon and Sayati Snow will demonstrate them for you in the morning, Chancellor. At first light."

"They know how to operate this . . . photon-director?"

"Yes. And they aided me immeasurably in their construction—there are three, you see. Three photon-directors. Apparently the Atarite inhibition against conceiving and developing an advanced weapon doesn't extend to mechanical matters like assembly and use, Chancellor Blaine."

"It's been rumored that I have Pelagan ancestors," Sayati Snow said. He was a man of my own age, a mathematician and abstruse theorist. His smile surprised me.

"And I," Master Gordon said, not smiling, "don't like being ruled by enzyme tags, plastic viruses, tampered-with chromosomes, any of that business. So I help with this." Gordon was an artisan, a stocky, dark-complexioned man with violet eyes.

"At first light, then," Chancellor Blaine said. He led the others to their rooms in the palace, and I found my own gloomy bachelor's quarters, deserted now since long before spring (with the exception of the nights I had spent there after bringing the Pelagan captive in from Stonelore), two rooms in the low building opposite the recreation hall. Amid the smells of musty quilts and stale air, I slept.

At first light Gordon and Snow demonstrated one of the photon-directors in the recreation hall. Gabriel Elk stood to one side, with Chancellor Blaine and me, and watched. While his terrible, sleek, streamlined machine burned holes of various shapes and sizes in several different target materials against one of the building's wall, the old man talked:

"The old name was laser," he said, "and oddly enough it was perfected on Earth *after* the weapon that twice—in Holocausts A and B—leveled the civilizations of mankind. That the Parfects chose even to hint at its existence suggests that they looked upon it as a device chiefly beneficial. Necessarily," he said, making the word sound evil, "we are going to pervert it to our own ends."

We watched as Sayati Snow triggered the device and a

beam of intense, ghastly red light shot through the hall and burned a hole in a cuirassed dummy suspended from the ceiling. Gordon turned a small wheel on the side of the machine's casing and manually directed the beam to inscribe a valentine on the cuirass' left breastplate. When he had finished, a heart-shaped plug of bronze smouldered there. For a long time the plug did not fall; it was as if the metal didn't even know that it had been severed from its own contoured matrix, the torso of our hay-filled warrior. This inscription the photon-director made without even setting the strawman afire. At last, realizing its separateness from the cuirass around it, the plug fell and rang hollowly on the stone floor. Then Sayati Snow triggered the machine again and a brief stream of ruby light ignited the effigy. The dummy burned madly, and the breastplate, no longer having anything to support it, dropped to the floor with a hot clang of its own.

From where we stood we could still feel the heat the machine had generated and the scalding backwind of the destroyed dummy.

Then, after a time, Blaine: "And these will save us?"

"Unless the Pelagans are more cunning monsters than we," Elk said. "I suggest that you send Master Gordon and Sayati Snow, each with a photon-director, to the front. Then, position each man on a flank of Field-Pavan Barrow's line of defense. Ingram and I, with the third machine, will go aboard a warship to the northern run—to halt the barbarians' supply fleet."

"Why not a direct assault on Orcland and the Pelagan capital?" Chancellor Blaine asked. "That would be surer. Much surer than trying to intercept the supply fleet in the White Sea fogs—with one vessel and a dubious weapon."

"The weapons are far from dubious, Chancellor, and I'm

requesting two escort vessels in addition to the warship carrying the machine itself. As for the *lasers*, they're to be used only defensively."

"And returned to you?"

"And returned to me."

"Very well, Sayati Elk."

That afternoon, accompanied by a guard of Atarite retainers, Gordon and Snow left Lunn for the northern provinces. Elk and I rode in an unguarded wagon to the little port of Brechtlin and there, as two old masker stevedores carried our boxed weapon aboard the warship *Paradise*, watched the landward gulls flashing their wings in the day's last light.

A seaman pointed out to Elk and me the stretch of beach where the widows, grandmothers, and spinsters from Lunn had waded into the indifferent water and drowned themselves.

xiv

We sailed in the morning. Around the southeastern cape of Ongladred we went, passing the village of Mershead and picking up an escort of two heavily armed galleons. The weather was good, the wind blew from the south, a late maloob, and our sails bellied out like so many linen-shirted paunches. For nearly fifty kilometers we followed Ongladred's coast, staying within the line of defensive warships positioned ten kilometers off the land at intervals just permitting each captain to see the vessels on his flanks; then we were swept out in the Angromain Channel and journeyed northward as a trinity of solitary freelancers, glorified reivers, our task the crippling of our enemy's supply efforts, a task we would have to accomplish amid an archipelago not of rocky, knife-edged islands but of glittering, tabular icebergs, all of them perilously in movement. Through the Angromain Run we sailed, into the cliff-littered White Sea.

On this trip Gabriel Elk taught me how to aim, activate, and control the beam of the photon-director, which we had mounted on the raised forward deck of the *Paradise*. I spent two hours one afternoon burning holes in the improvised sails of a dinghy being dragged at a safe distance behind one of our companion vessels; then I sank the dinghy, setting both its sails and hull ablaze. The sailors on the *Sea Drake* cut the little boat's tow line and waved cheerily at me. I think I grinned. The maskers at Stonelore had never reacted with even half the effusiveness of the seamen; not once. Those on the *Mandragora*, our other companion, even fired a cannon. How much more powerful than this could one feel, I wondered.

"Good, Ingram," Gabriel Elk said. "Soon you'll use your new-found skills against the Pelagans."

"Me? Why not you, Sayati Elk?"

"I've done enough, Ingram. This is for you."

We did not talk about how Snow and Gordon were faring nor about how the forces of Field-Pavan Barrow were acquitting themselves. These were things out of our control. We could only hope that the Pelagans had not altered their manner of supplying their own forces and that we could intercept them in the White Sea. But although we didn't talk about the land war, it wasn't hard to see that Elk frequently thought of it. In more than one sense, his own blood struggled in that conflict, strove both to honor itself and to pulse for its nation—even though the old man and his son were driven more by abstract ideals than by any fanatic nationalism.

The wind continued brisk, and on our third evening at sea we entered the southernmost reach of the Angromain Run, that corridor of indigo- and vermilion-shot water between Ongladred's northern coast and the overarching scorpion's tail of the barbarian archipelago. Most of these islands are little more than rocks, and uninhabited. Of our voyage into this region I remember principally the bitterness of the night air and, off to port, the small, pearl-like fires burning on the coast. These were now and again visible when a jut of land, like the nub of a gigantic finger, poked out accusingly from our island-nation's usually unobtrusive shore. Parallel to Firthshir Province's eastern coast, we saw no more of these fires; the enemy had let them go out—apparently they did not fear the sloak, or had forgotten about it, or (the most likely alternative) had insufficient men to keep the fires going.

But even without the coastal bonfires the *Paradise* sailed on a mirror surface of rich, darkly rich light; the Shattered Moons illuminated the Angromain Run as if it were a floor of marble and swirled the icy water with deeper indigos, more elusive vermilions. Was it really true that in the wake of the Pelagan advance our country was becoming a gutted ashpit? At sea, it did not seem possible, for the moonlight had an aurora-like brilliance and the very air sparkled. At night I spent as much time as I could on the *Paradise*'s decks, just to see these things—the immemorial wheeling of stars, and of water, and of curdled satellites.

"The moons are brighter out here," I told Elk on our third night.

"One or several of them are artificial," he said.

"How do you know that, Sayati Elk?"

"The Parfects carried us out here six thousand years ago, carried us out here eight hundred light-years from Earth. At least one of the Shattered Moons, perhaps the minutest shard, is an instrument of observation, data-accumulation, and relay—the Eyes and Ears of the neo-people who attempted to re-engineer their own progenitors. Mankind was given genes for morality. You and I, then, are integers in a modestly cosmic experiment, Ingram, and the Parfects therefore have a small vested interest in us—they would have wanted to see how their experiment turned out, they would have made provision for monitoring this hemisphere of Mansueceria, at least."

"But how do you—?"

"It doesn't stop there. They would have wanted a means of interfering in our affairs, of altering the balance of historical forces in Ongladred—if the need arose. Their satellite or satellites among the Shattered Moons fulfill this purpose, too."

"Robin Coigns told me once that he believed the Parfects would return and repair our botched world at the third coming of the sloak. Surely you don't believe that, Sayati Elk?"

"No, Ingram. One property that we can't lease out is the equivocal terrain of our fates."

"An epigram," I said with a cruel inflection that surprised even me.

"If you like, Ingram. But true for all that. In spite of the Parfects, we're alone, and we are also accountable."

"But this instrument in the sky, the Eyes and Ears of the Parfects, how can you be so certain it exists? What proof have you?"

Sayati Elk looked up at the curling, night-darkened sails; then, grinning like a sly adolescent, he said, "Faith. Simple faith, Ingram." And he went down from the forward deck to his own private cabin.

On our fourth morning we were in the White Sea, traveling northwest out of the Angromain Run. Since we had no idea into which of the many sinuous fjords at the top of Ongladred the Pelagans were running their supplies, our little fleet stood well out to sea and waited. Eventually the barbarians' hideous ships would have to sweep down the arc of the Angromain's scorpion's tail and reveal themselves—or else, for want of provisions, our invaders would soon have to plump out their bellies on ash and gunpowder. Several kilometers out from the coast we tacked about and faced to the east, our three vessels now strategically placed and separated in order to cover the wide, white mouth of water out of which our enemy must sail, dragon-prowed and sinister. *Evil* was the word I thought, knowing that Sayati Elk would have merely laughed at the literalness of my imagination.

We had nothing to do but wait. Nothing but wait and watch the icebergs drift down from Mansueceria's polar cap, sedate and reflective—like hermetically sealed, buoyant cities of crystal. Or like imperturbable monsters of glass.

We saw five icebergs on our first day of waiting, none so close that it posed a danger to the *Paradise* but all near enough to incite our wonder. The closest to us had inlets and firths like an island, although its sides rose up from the White Sea so steeply that none of these afforded a landing place; an eerie sucking roar emanated from the iceberg's caves as the sea rushed in, and a reverberant echo followed each guttural shout. The ice itself was a thousand different colors, mostly shades of blue that purpled the water beneath the iceberg and, as the evening drew on, turned the sky behind it a brittle cobalt. Maz went down early, but not before we saw this nearest leviathan calve and heard the thunderous groanings of her birth pangs as the ice tore apart. Another night to wait, but our first night to worry about ramming the progeny of a multicolored and fecund ice-creature.

Captain Chant, apparently, had seen service in the White Sea before, and we survived the night intact.

The fifth morning greeted us with cottony banks of fog, all of it rolling down from the archipelago's last few islands. The *Sea Drake* and *Mandragora* disappeared, faded away into the gathering gauze as we watched—like apparitions becoming once more invisible. We were enshrouded, we were made a bobbing universe to ourselves. Now our fears were that the icebergs would demolish us or, even worse, that the Pelagans would glide by us in the murk.

Again, we could do nothing but wait, muffled in this hanging fog. Maz was a wan dream somewhere on the other side of our anxiety, and fog drooped down on us from the masts and spars like a ghostly moss. Then night fell, a night that sealed us into ourselves.

All that reminded us of the worlds beyond our own was the intermittent ringing of the *Sea Drake*'s and the *Mandragora*'s ships' bells. The bells' notes, blurred by the fog, drifted through the darkness to us like parachutes of iron sound. Where did they come from? How did they reach us? And then I realized that the *Paradise* had a bellman of its own, that he was on the forward deck (by Gabriel Elk's canvas-covered machine), and that our bell, too, occasionally sent out peals of hollow warning.

"Aren't we just giving ourselves away to the Pelagans?" I asked a masker seaman on the *Paradise*'s main deck. I nodded forward.

"Oh, the bell. Perhaps, Master. But it's better than banging up against our sister ships, and the Pelagans—if they're out in this—have most likely ceased to run, so as to let the soup blow off. They've got fellows with passable heads, too, you know."

I said: "Our bells won't keep the icebergs off. They don't listen."

"If we bump we bump, Master. It may mean giving up a sail or two, but we'll pull her by. So, too, the *Drake* and the *Mandragora*."

His confidence was pleasant but not contagious. I went below decks and tried to sleep.

XV

On the sixth morning the fog was shredding. Shredding
into a series of staggered curtains, some of them standing
open, some of them closed but for a hairline of blue where
sea and sky parted them. Our sister ships became visible
once more. Ahead of us, still partially veiled, the mouth of
White Sea water from which our enemy would have to come.
Feebly Maz was parting the veils, revealing the icy glitter,
the stretch of predatory sea, that had been curtained from us.

A voice cried out: "Dragons floating! Six in flight!"

Gabriel Elk came by me, wrapped in furs. Sailors began
moving on the *Paradise's* decks.

Paralyzed, I watched, watched everything.

In a crush of moving bodies the old man halted, twisted
his wide face toward me, said, "Up here, Ingram, up here,"

and strode purposefully through the swarming men, a distinct and preeminent figure. I watched him climb to the forward deck. His stocky form teetered above me, disappeared. Then it was at the head of the ladder again, gazing down on me—though I couldn't see the old man's eyes, only the light pouring down over his shoulders and through his akimbo arms. "Ingram, get up here, damn you! Is all the fog in your head now?" These words overmastered the confusion; somehow, though spoken in an almost conversational tone, they were audible.

In only a moment I was beside Gabriel Elk.

Looking forward over the prow of the *Paradise* I saw nothing—nothing but twinkling water and, slightly to our left, a single iceberg. No other icebergs were visible, only this one rectangular block whose length was several times that of our ship's. It loomed, loomed just out of our intended course. Again, the cry from aloft: "Dragons floating! Six in flight!" And I wondered if the man up there weren't simply reading his own apprehensions into the facets of this solitary iceberg. Maybe the dragons floated in his mind, nowhere else.

"There," Elk said, pointing, and I saw the sail: the first sail.

It seemed to rise up out of the White Sea like the wings of a pelagic, half-frozen pterodactyl, crisp and crimson-brown. Fog scattered as these wings beat through. The prow rising up beneath the Pelagan vessel's sail was carven into the shape of a horned, reptilian head—like that of a dragon, or a fire-lizard, or even an ancient Earth saurian. Exact identification hardly mattered. The impression was that of the entire ship's having emerged hungry from a long sleep in the cold sea. Now the monster was hunting, and the only prey in its path was the galleon on whose forward deck I stood.

One by one the other five sails breasted the horizon, popped into view as if propelled upward from the White Sea's bottom. We saw them, they saw us. And the other five

Pelagan ships were as hideously accoutred as the first, bright banners streaming above their dried-blood-colored sails.

On the *Paradise* orders were called out. Gabriel Elk tenderly and quickly drew the piece of padded canvas off the photon-director. It hit me that I was going to operate the machine, I was going to trigger it, I was going to control the intensity and the direction of its scorching needle-flare. More orders were called out; I didn't know where or from whom. The old man said something to me, bumped me into place. My gloved hands were on the photon-director's obscenely neutral-looking controls, a curved trigger and a simple metal wheel. And out in front of me: water like frozen milk, a single bluey-green berg drifting toward us several hundred meters away, and the distance-dwindled but still terrifying Pelagan warships. The only fog I saw now was peripheral, every wispy curtain drawn into the wings of our theatre of battle. Inside my heavy gloves my hands were sweating.

"Are we in range?" I somehow asked, the words atremble with two different kinds of cold, my voice hoarse as if from shouting.

Elk said, "Only a target beneath the horizon is safe, Ingram."

"Do I fire?"

"Did you hear Captain Chant?"

I looked at the old man—at his face under the fur cap, at the iceberg-green eyes, at the snowy sideburns standing away from his cheeks. How long had I known him? Why was he talking to me?

Quietly, guardedly, he was saying, "Captain Chant wants you to wait—to see if they'll turn now that they've seen us, turn and go home." *Was this true?*

Absently I said, "I didn't hear that order."

Then, from aft, I heard a megaphoned command. "Commence firing, Master Marley. COMMENCE FIRING!" The order echoed aloft, the air reverberated with it, the immense northern sea swallowed the echo.

Gabriel Elk pushed me away from the mounted machine, pinioned my arms. "Captain Chant, Captain Chant, I've decided that this man will fire at my word! At no other word but my own!" Then he released me and shoved me back into place.

My hands gravitated to the laser's controls—and I was very conscious of the sharp rippling of the highest foresails. My gums burned with the otherworldly chill, my ears throbbed acutely, and the *Paradise* seemed frozen by Sayati Elk's legitimate, but irregular, usurpation of the galleon-captain's command role. No one moved. Captain Chant's megaphone was stilled.

The Pelagan's little supply fleet had indeed begun to turn—but not out of either fear or surprise. Two of the dragon-prowed ships were maneuvering away from the other four, off to the west. The remainder continued to run toward us, but with their starboard hulls slightly open to us and cutting across the wind. Like ours, the ships were all three-masted, but the sails differed from ours in being serrated and ornamented. Each topgallant bore the yin-yang symbol which Elk had once told me the barbarians had appropriated from legendary Cathay. I stared as ships and sails alike came on.

"Do you know what to do, Ingram?"

I nodded. I could tear cloth with the photon-director, I could burn clean holes, I could set lacerating fires, I could incinerate men on deck, I could sear off mastheads, I could open ragged vents beneath the ships' water lines. What could I not do?

—Turn the barbarians back with a shouted word, with a wave of the hand. No hope of that; none.

Therefore, I would wield Elk's re-created machine as if it were a funnel for all my frustration and rage.

"For Maz' sake, Sayati Elk," Captain Chant called out from the pilot's deck, "let the young master fire!"

"Stay your hand yet," the old man whispered fiercely in my ear.

Numb, I obeyed. I saw a puff of smoke appear as if by magic on the starboard side of the foremost Pelagan vessel. Momentarily I feared that I had triggered my weapon by mistake. The puff of smoke tattered into greasy threads and blew away on the wind; a roar followed, pinched-sounding at this distance. Then, about fifty meters out to sea, a spout of water suddenly kicked up in front of the *Paradise;* air and water vibrated with the shock. It was as if someone had poured liquid mercury into my ears, that painfully deafening.

Another puff of smoke, followed rapidly by another; two muted barks in succession; then the shock of impact as the milky sea broke under the weight of Pelagan cannon shot and water spiraled up in two separate fountains off our bow. I could see individual drops glistering in the midmorning air, miniature prisms tracing their own kaleidoscopic parabolas of descent. Altogether numb, I watched.

"Sayati Elk!" Captain Chant was shouting. "Let him fire!"

"Fire, then," the old man said in my ear.

I pulled the trigger with my gloved finger, then released it. The machine's needle-flare blazed out over the White Sea like a radiant, resilient thread snapping from one point to another—as if its light had originated at the target point and then simply reeled the instantaneous beam out of the photon-director's tubular throat: *Ffffffthup!* An obscene, rapid sucking. Afterwards the air seemed changed—but the beam itself shot past the enemy warship; was bewilderingly absorbed by the changed, electrically cold air.

Had my finger touched off this raylike lightning, this gone-astray miracle of fire?

Bursts of smoke formed and dissolved on the sides of two

of the Pelagan warships; spray kicked up all across the bow of the *Paradise,* the noise was almost insupportable, water leapt up to us on the high forward deck so that we were drenched with its lashing fallout.

"Again, Ingram!" Elk shouted at me. "Again!"

I swiveled the laser on its mount, I pressed the trigger and held it back with all my will. Rage, frustration, bewilderment, longing for power, impotence, hatred, pride—these and more spun out of me in the swift embodiment of the photon-director's luminous, ruby ray. Almost blinded, I swiveled the machine, turned the wheel controlling the beam, and, teeth achingly clamped, willed the disintegration of everything that was not Ingram Marley.

I stitched the sails of the first Pelagan ship with fire, I sheered off all three masts above their topgallants, I scorched a line of black piping along the middle of its starboard hull. There were drops of water on my eyelashes, tears of half-frozen spray, and the red lambency of the emotions streaming out through the tube of the photon-director was reflected a thousand excruciating times in these tiny beads of ice.

The cannon aboard the first Pelagan ship ceased firing; no more innocent-looking puffballs of smoke. Aboard the *Paradise* we could hear men screaming, men shrieking like the winter ghost-wind. Their full-voiced terror was ludicrously out of phase with the placidity of the northern sea.

We could hear the splintering crack of wood; we could see the severed mastheads toppling, catching, and ultimately tearing through the adjacent sails to crash against the warship's decks, indiscriminately crushing men and equipment alike. The hull of the Pelagan ship was filling with water and ineluctably beginning to capsize—sails hanging and aflame, banners altogether scorched away, the dragon-prow glaring balefully out of one burnt-out eye and nodding ever seaward.

Finally I released the trigger, stopped swiveling the photon-director.

The booming of cannon growled over the water again, but this time from the *Mandragora,* which lay a little behind us and over a hundred meters to our right. A hollow booming, full of antiquated fury. Spray began geysering up in front of the enemy vessel that I had already effectively demolished, a line of violent punctuation marks. They added nothing at all to the unequivocal statement of the photon-director.

"They're jumping," Gabriel Elk said. "The Pelagan seamen who are still able to, Ingram, are jumping. They won't last ten minutes in the White Sea. If that long." The old man was not looking at me, but at the sinking warship. "If that long," he reiterated.

I remembered something. "Where's the *Sea Drake?*"

"There." He gestured off to port. "Those two warships that split away from the main contingent are bearing down on her, trying to use that iceberg as a screen between her and us."

They were moving west, but because of our position I had to look north to see them. Already they had got behind the iceberg's striated, azure-and-rose cliffs and, in a moment, were cannonading the *Sea Drake*—a cacophonous, echoing barrage. At the same time, the three remaining vessels assaulting us and our other companion continued to come on, undeterred by the demolition of their leader or the ungodly shrieking of half its crew. Apparently no effort was being made to pick up the overboarded sailors; the Pelagans knew what Gabriel Elk knew, that they were dead men. Three warships, then, bore down on us; their two fellows attacked the *Sea Drake.*

Captain Chant was shouting orders again; masker seamen scrambled about frantically on the *Paradise's* main deck.

I was drained, trembling.

"What should I do now, Sayati Elk?"

"Take the ones closing in on us, Ingram. I see nothing else for it."

Swiveling the photon-director, I aimed at the Pelagan vessel negotiating its way toward us from behind the wreckage of the first. In ten minutes I had reduced it to a smouldering shell, masts down, hull precisely stove in. More men were in the water, and smoke trailed away to the north like a tattered banner. Even through my gloves I could feel the heat coming off the casing of Elk's machine. Inside my fur clothes I was sweating, profusely sweating. My face felt hot—but in my eyelashes, those frozen beads in which I could see the distorted reflections of the scene before me! No longer was I firing out of rage, or frustration, or hate; cold resolve sustained me, that and Sayati Elk's droning, almost perfunctory encouragement. For these things I had created wreckage.

"Now the third, Ingram; now the third."

I destroyed the third ship, even though it had finally begun to turn away from the conflict; its captain had witnessed enough. No doubt he died with a terror in his heart more dreadful than that his ship's painted sails and grotesque dragon-prow had ever provoked in his enemies.

The fourth Pelagan warship fled. Successfully.

"Let it go, Ingram. Let it go. Someone must carry word of this back to the archipelago, back to Orcland."

Off to port, off to the northwest, the *Sea Drake* was suffering the methodical onslaught of the barbarian ships shielded by the now seemingly immobile iceberg. Their cannonade continued. The booming was deceptively melodic, deep and sweet. We could already see, however, that the *Sea Drake* would not survive the encounter; its foremost and several of its staysails were down, and she was returning fire only rarely, a tacit acknowledgment of her doom. Neither the *Paradise* nor the *Mandragora* had taken a direct hit.

"Can you help her?" Captain Chant shouted.

"Can we?" I asked.

"If you can burn through that berg, Ingram, if you can split it up and give yourself an aisleway to your targets."

"Can I do that?"

"Probably not. I don't know. Its volume may be too great."

Again, I swiveled the laser on its mount. Again, I adjusted the intensity and width of its beam, allowing for maximums in both. Again, I pulled the trigger back and held it in place.

At once the iceberg erupted in an almost volcanic billowing of steam, white clouds pouring over its table-top and sweeping off like thin gas. Hissing and creaking accompanied this eruption. When I finally released the trigger, the photondirector had done little more than bore an uneven tunnel whose depth I couldn't gauge.

Ships fell to this weapon more readily than did the calves of Mansueceria's polar cap. Still—with time—I might have won through. It was just that we didn't have the time. . . .

The *Sea Drake*, gently capsizing into a foam scarcely whiter than the surrounding sea, slid out of our sight; gently she went, incredibly gently. If her crewmen were screaming, we did not hear them. Maskers often die without even a sigh of protest, and the officers of Ongladred, the Atarite elite, must emulate their stoicism, even in death. We watched our sister ship go down, we watched her slide with broken but commanding dignity into the indigo-riven deeps. And all on the *Paradise* were silent, stilled by our comrades' last end.

"Wait for the bastards," the old man told me. "Wait for them, Ingram, until they have to pull out."

Fetched up with the *Mandragora*, we waited, we waited for the Pelagan renegades to sail out from behind the iceberg. I am certain that they knew we were waiting, that they had seen what we had done to the rest of their fleet.

A half-hour went by, then forty-five minutes. And when the barbarian ships came out they came out on opposite sides of the azure-and-rose ice plateau, cannons booming, their captains apparently determined that one crew would sacrifice itself for the other.

The water was pockmarked with shot, deliquescent with spray.

"Incinerate them," Gabriel Elk said. His voice was flat.

Working first on one ship, then on the other, I did just that. I alternated until they both went down, blackened husks crumbling into ash on the waters. We were not hit. When it was over, Gabriel Elk stalked away from me, descended to the main deck, strode the length of the ship, and without a word to anyone ducked into the passageway leading to his cabin.

I looked on my work: the sinking ruins; the flotsam of boards, boxes, and men bent double like shrimp-things, all bobbing hopelessly in the White Sea; and the smoke curling and dissolving above it all.

Then, the photon-director. On its swivel it sat: a slender, single-eyed beast no more remorseful than the snake that strikes and soon afterwards sleeps. I covered it with a piece of canvas. That way I could continue to look at it.

I looked at it for a long time.

xvi

That evening as we sailed southward, the sky still smoking behind us and the *Mandragora*'s masts and sails silhouetted against that sky's brownish flame, I went below decks. I knocked on the door of Gabriel Elk's cabin. He had not been seen after our victory over the Pelagans; he had not joined Captain Chant and the other Atarite officers in the mess. So I went to Sayati Elk's cabin, and knocked.

"It's open," he called, his voice still disconcertingly flat.

He was sitting on a stool in the middle of the small room, and over him leaned a middle-aged masker seaman with a razor. A basin of sudsy water rested on the writing surface next to Elk's bunk. The masker, a thin little fellow with no eyebrows, was shaving Elk; he grinned at me when I opened the door, then went back to work.

"This is Gnot," the old man said. "Yukio Gnot. He's a barber as well as a yard-trimmer and buntline-tender."

I squeezed past the two men and sat down on the narrow cabin's bunk, a sort of wall cot. The little masker bowed. The hand holding the razor was extended gallantly out behind him. He recited,

> *"I am Gnot, the man*
> *You think I am,"*

and resumed work for a second time; all this he did completely humorlessly, with dead-pan seriousness in fact.

Elk was wrapped to the throat in a khaki-colored apron, his face partially lathered, unnaturally pink where Gnot had already shaved him. Then I noticed that on the desk next to me, as well as the barber's soap-filled basin, there was a pair of heavy shears. What did all this mean?

For a time we listened to the groanings of the *Paradise:* Elk in his khaki tent, Gnot concentratingly ignoring the sway of the ship, and I somehow excluded from the intimacy of shaver and shaved. Between groanings I thought I could hear the almost frictionless scraping of Gnot's razor; it was as if the razor were scraping at the wet inside of my skull.

Would no one speak?

"I'm sorry I deserted you, Ingram," Gabriel Elk said. "I'm sorry I made you do what I made you do."

"You did desert me, didn't you?"

"Yes. But no more certainly than I deserted myself after we closed Stonelore—and created again that thing out there."

"That was for a cause, Sayati Elk. What about this morning's desertion? What about leaving me?"

"For the cause of my own sanity, Ingram. As the gold-hearted beauty of the Stews once said, 'It's nothing personal, Master, nothing personal a' tall.' But I regret the desertion mightily for what it seemed to imply."

"Why are you being shaved at this hour?"

"An ablution of sorts," puckering his mouth as Yukio Gnot scraped at the grizzled whiskers near his Adam's apple. "Perhaps I should be bled clean. Gentleman Gnot, an extra mithra if you go into the jugular neatly."

The masker stepped back. "There's nothing neat about that operation, Sayati Elk. As for the mithra, I'm Gnot for nothing and all's for Gnot in this barbering. You owe me nothing, for all the pleasure's mine." It was patter, amusing but sadly hollow. The little man leaned over Gabriel Elk again, his browless eyes naked and vulnerable—like ripe, peeled grapes.

His hands flashed expertly. Then I saw that he was shaving away Elk's sideburns.

I said, "Gentleman Gnot, was that requested?"

Elk threw me a sidelong look, the whites of his eyeballs like little quarter moons. "All of it's requested, Ingram. Jaw, cheeks, and skull. All of it."

"The masker mourning cap," I said. "What for?"

"For today."

"You aren't one of the People Accustomed to the Hand," I said, "and you haven't lost a relative. Did you do this when your two eldest sons died?"

"I didn't, Ingram—because I wasn't a Mansuecerian, though born of them, and their customs weren't mine. Today I revive the custom of the mourning cap. Why? Because I mourn and don't know how to express it, the expression of it's gone out of me, all of it out. Today was a day I relearned everything but its expression, Ingram, and so I turned to Gentleman Gnot for help. I'm no longer young, I'm nearing death, in fact—but I've never understood the element of affirmation that may exist in mourning, though I know that it *does* exist.

"The Atarite practice of mourning has always struck me as

defeatist; the Mansuecerian, as cold and ritualized. But to-day—a day of my own making—requires this atonement at least. Already a kind of feeling flows in, behind Good Barber Gnot's fashioning of my cap. The outside will teach the inside. What say you to that, Ingram?"

"Nothing. Nonsense from Our Genius."

"Exhibitionist nonsense?"

"Your words, your doubts."

The old man shifted under the khaki barber's cloth. The wall candles flickered together; the cabin filled with interlocking shadows, most of them pooling and ebbing around the two men in the center of the room. Delicately Yukio Gnot wiped the lather from Gabriel Elk's face; the old man's face was then naked, as if newborn. I wondered if I would have been able to recognize Elk if I had not seen the transformation. "I'm a dramatist and poet," he said confidently. "Introspection and exhibitionism have been my trades. No doubts whatever in that, Ingram. This that I do now has nothing to do with my trades, however. It has to do with my humanity and mortality. How the world interprets it, I little care."

He gestured at the spry, shadow-tattered barber and said, "Proceed."

Gnot took the heavy shears off the cabin's writing desk (I had to move my feet for him) and began sclip-sclipping at Elk's massive head, the ring-curled, silver-white hair tumbling over the shears' blades like wool. Satyr's wool, I thought: Elk was smiling cryptically. Like the parings of old dreams the hair fell. In the shadow-filled cabin it almost floated, each curl a fleck of time, of coil-wound chronology, cut and discarded. Individual hairs clung to the drab bib or laced the floor with their dead, frightening beauty. I could not help thinking that this was something more than a simple barbering: I thought of the Parfects, I thought of the Pelagan reiver I had murdered, I thought of denatured animals and the resurrected performers of Stonelore. A sense of elation; a sense of loss. And the hair kept curling away from the blade, emphatically white.

When Gnot had finished with the shears, he lathered Gabriel Elk's shorn head, stropped his razor, and began scraping away the stubble. "Harvest time," Elk said. He sat perfectly still under the little masker's hands. Then, the operation complete, Gnot laid the shears aside and washed his patient's liver-spotted skull. Strangely, Elk did not look ludicrous—maybe because his bald head didn't shine like a tunic button, but more probably because his face, in its runneled candor, green eyes hemmed in like a tortoise's, was already humorous at its own expense.

"Done, Sayati Elk. You needn't pay me. I'm Gnot for nothing."

"I'd rather, Gnot," Gabriel Elk said, shaking the apron out on the floor and giving the barber a few coins.

The barber bowed; he grinned. "Oh, that's amusing, Sayati Elk, that's amusing how you put that. I'm appreciative, I am."

I said, "I'm doubled with laughter myself, tied up in a Gnot."

"Oh, Master Marley," he said, looking at me, "you, too. You, too. All's for Gnot, it is. All's for Gnot."

In disgust, I looked at the floor.

"I'll clean up, Gnot," Elk said. "You needn't feel obligated for that, too. You're a seaman and a barber, not a mercenary in the broom brigade." This time the *not* wasn't a pun; the old man's voice had changed.

"Oh, no. I must do it, you know." He took a small horsehair brush from the inside of his jacket, knelt, and swept the fallen hair into the barber's apron, which he had spread out on the floor as a receptacle for hair, dust, and any other oddments he could rake together. Speedily done, he pulled the four corners of the apron together and tied them up as best he could, careful not to spill either dirt or severed curls. He slung the resulting bag over his shoulder. He bowed to Gabriel Elk; he bowed to me. He looked like an archetypal gift-bringer, but one whose generosity has dissipated him into a posturing—and anemic—clown.

"Take a few of those shavings," I suggested, "and paste on some eyebrows."

The masker, alerted to something *unkind* in my tone, stared at me in utter incomprehension; his nonexistent eyebrows were quizzically raised. Elk opened the cabin door for him, let him into the hall.

"Thank you, Yukio," I could hear him saying. "You're a skillful man, and a good one. Let's hope we find our country and families safe when we put in at Brechtlin."

"Yes, Sayati Elk. Let's so hope."

Elk returned to the cabin. He sat down opposite me, pulling his stool around as he sat. His naked, gravely humorous face was as unfamiliar as a map of Austernmere, the Brobdingnagian continent sprawling over a quarter of Mansueceria's southern hemisphere. The naked, unfamiliar face looked at me, simply looked at me.

At last I said, "Oh, that wasn't so bad, Sayati Elk. I've sunk five ships today, drowned nearly eight hundred men in an icy sea. Insulting Gentleman Gnot was one of my less murderous sallies of the day." I wanted to cry. Instead, I pulled in my bottom lip and tried—tried very hard—to stare the old bastard down.

"A Mansuecerian, Ingram. A simple masker—"

"Why are you trying to shame me?"

"Oh no, Ingram, I don't mean to shame you, just to explain that his shaving my head was my idea, not his. To explain that he speaks as he does because he's a simple, untouched creature."

"But the banality of it, Sayati Elk, the endless banality of it." And my eyes filled with wet candlelight, diamonds of melting, detonating color that washed the old man's unfamiliar face away. I couldn't control my shoulders. *"The terrible, utter banality . . ."*

Then I could smell the old man's lather-sour warmth, feel his heavy arm and strong hand pulling me like a child into his side; he was sitting on the bunk next to me, a reality that had swum through my blurred vision to assert its realness. The voice was warm against my face. "It's a banality which touches us all, Ingram—and we all attempt to transcend it, in whatever ways we're able. Even Yukio Gnot. Even the maskers who come to Stonelore." His huge hand squeezed my biceps. "But for pushing you to this, I'm sorry. My mourning is for you, too."

"Will what we've done make a damn bit of difference?"

"That's hard to gauge."

"Won't the Pelagans send more ships, and more, and more?"

"One escaped today. That one will return to Orcland, and the news its captain gives of his compatriots' end will soon be broadcast throughout the archipelago, both as rumor and warning. Or so I hope."

I pulled away from the old man. In the melting-diamond light I found my feet and crossed to the door. "Goodnight, Sayati Elk." I went out without waiting for his reply. Inside my fur-lined parka my shoulders became a part of my body again, settled almost comfortably into me.

In the cold I found my way to the forward deck. There I directed two masker seamen to take the photon-director off its mount and carry it to my cabin. Under close-hauled sails, tarnished-tin stars, and the shadow-pocked moons, they did so.

They put the machine on the floor in the center of my cabin, and I sat on the edge of my bunk for a long time looking at it. Then I extinguished my lamps, undressed in the dark, and lay down under several ragged quilts.

(Pulling them up, I remembered a quilt with blue flowers embroidered over its silken squares.)

The *Paradise* groaned, gently rocking. The shadow of the photon-director, the sinister bulking of its silhouette, drew my attention, and I stared at it as if compelled to wrestle with the implications of its shape. I was past crying. I lay in the dark and relived the morning and early afternoon, oh, eight or a thousand times. Then was rocked into dreamless nightmare, a series of floating images without correlatives. . . .

xvii

On the morning that we rounded the southeastern cape of Ongladred, a strange thing happened. Captain Chant was wringing the very air for wind, so motionlessly still was the day; our sails were expertly trimmed, the yards finically dressed, and we were moving homeward—but only just. The *Paradise* rode the shallow, almost nonexistent waves sluggishly, and the *Mandragora* had fallen back half a kilometer in our languid wake. Aloft, our banners scarcely fluttered.

Because the sailing was so poor along our island's coast, we rounded the Mershead Cape well out to sea—far enough out so that land was no longer visible. Although we were now in waters lapping quiescently against uninvaded terri-

131

tory (the civilized heartland of our nation), we saw only five or six ships of all of Ongladred's fleet, and all of these out of hailing distance.

It was an odd morning, a subdued and lonely sort of homecoming.

Gabriel Elk and I stood with Captain Chant and his helmsman on the pilot's deck. Maz shone with a thin but elemental vigor; He did not seem a likely one to nova, to explode us all back into primordial plasma. Therefore none of us wore parkas or overtunics; we basked in the uncommon autumn mildness. And wondered at the absence of wind and the tranquility of the sea.

"Where are all our ships, Sayati Elk?" I asked.

"On a day like this," Captain Chant answered, "their captains would hope to be in harbor. Perhaps that's where they are today."

"But we ought to see a few. A precaution against the Pelagans."

"The Pelagans, Ingram," the old man said, "are defeated. I know it. Last night—and the night before—we saw the bonfires on the coast. Having beat back one enemy, our people are turning their energies again to the threat of the sloak. Like Captain Chant, I believe most of our ships to be in harbor."

"But the sloak," I said, "is no threat at all; a superstition."

"Perhaps not a superstition," Gabriel Elk said. His uncovered head struck me again as shamefully naked, a violation of character. Captain Chant's eyes caught mine once and their irises seemed to surround a question.

But our desultory talk continued. Meanwhile, on the *Paradise*'s decks our sailors worked with quiet, insectlike efficiency keeping the sails open to whatever breath of wind they could smell or intuit in the listless air. We were bound for home, we were bound for home, and only that mattered.

The strange thing that happened that morning came too late to be an ironic comment on my refusal to see the sloak as a threat; too much time had passed to underscore my words with irony. Or so I tried to convince myself.

This is what happened:

Suddenly, with no warning, the sea beneath the *Paradise*—and everywhere else around us, insofar as we could judge—began to heave and surge, surge and heave, lifting and dropping in great, vaguely peristaltic swells. Our masker seamen turned their faces to the skies in disbelief, shouting to one another, checking braces and halyards. Captain Chant roared unintelligible orders over their shouts and scufflings, his megaphone jutting out before him like a supernatural trumpet. Officers on the other decks trumpeted these misheard orders back and forth over the sailors' heads, and the whole ship was atremble and ajostle with split-struck confusion.

Great slappings of water pounded our hull. It was as if a team of ocean-breathing giants—seaweed for beards and driftwood for bucklers—were playing at toss-the-blanket on the bottom of the Angromain Channel, oblivious to depth and pressure as impediments to their play. The flap-and-fall of their monumentally water-logged blanket translated itself into the lift-and-plunge that we aboard the *Paradise* were experiencing, into the running swells everywhere around us. It had to be giants. Since there was no wind, since our banners were still hardly billowing, this quaking of the sea, this ferocious faulting, had to originate from *beneath* the surface. I think that even I realized that, even I was aware of the odd nature of the channel's intransigence—and could do nothing but pray that the giants grow weary and desist. But, with Sayati Elk, I remained on deck, watching.

"The sloak!" I heard a voice cry out.

"Aye, the sloak!" in answer.

"The sloak it is!"

"The sloak!"

I grabbed Gabriel Elk's arm and shouted, "I don't believe that! This is some kind of tidal anomaly, isn't it?" I had to repeat my words, but I got the old man to face me.

"I've never seen a tide like this, Ingram!"

"What about sea-bottom volcanic activity?"

"Who can say, Master? Who can say?" He was reveling in the surge of the waters, the cry and scuffle of our sailors. Me, he had no immediate concern for; I couldn't question him while this untoward pounding made our bilge echo and our masts passionately thrust and fall back. Men were mocked in this, their tenderness and pride both mercilessly battered, and the old man laughed and drank it all in. Every haughty wave.

I shouted, "Do you—do you believe it's the sloak?"

But he didn't answer me, refused to hear me. Beside him on the pilot's deck I waited for an immense mythical creature to capsize and drown us on a transcendently fair day. The masker seamen, hauling line and climbing, kept us afloat, and then, in a split-struck instant, the seas calmed and the *Paradise* settled into a gently bobbing element scarcely even foam-flecked. The giants had wearied of blanket toss and gone on to more delicate amusements.

—*Like subduing boarnoses to their clammy hands*, I thought. I could imagine the sleek, sharklike creatures undergoing training.

After we had ridden for a time on the freshly stilled waters, I began to force my questions on the old man. We stayed abovedecks in the midmorning sun, a little away from Chant and his helmsman. "Was that really the sloak, Sayati Elk? Not freak vulcanism nor a quirk of the tides, but this creature you and the maskers call the sloak?"

"I believe so, Ingram."

"Why?"

"Because that answer, to my mind, is the only one that truly works, the simplest and most legitimate."

"Then do you expect this gelatinous monster to smother the coastal bonfires—haul itself irresistibly over our island—and destroy Ongladred for a third time? That seems to be all we can hope for?"

"Ingram, I am past expectation. Past prophecy and vision. But I don't think Ongladred will be destroyed again. At least not by an entity as remorselessly out-of-nature as the sloak."

"If you believe in the thing, why not?"

"Because what we've just experienced, Ingram, was meant as caveat and warning, it was directed specifically at us aboard this ship and the men on shore who witnessed the turbulence's batterings, the men of our nation."

"Caveat and warning," I said incredulously. "From whom? The sloak?"

"No, but from those who control it. It's a thing out-of-nature, Ingram, an anomaly in its own right, a product of smug and juridic intelligence. It has no will of its own; it executes the judgments of this 'higher,' all-ruling intelligence and does so in the guise of an apocalyptic but wholly natural phenomenon. The sloak exists, Ingram, but it's a lie."

"I don't understand you." —Although this argument was somehow familiar. I had heard it before. In Stonelore. From a haggish old woman in one of Elk's neuro-dramas.

"I'm speaking of the Parfects. The sloak is a quasi-organic creature, a biological construct which the Parfects have twice before activated in order to pull us back from forbidden knowledge. For them, the Old Knowledge is the limit of what we may know; the sloak, the unweaponlike weapon by which they fix the parameters of our knowledge. Once again, Ingram, we begin to encroach on the boundaries of the permitted: We have employed technology—proscribed technology—to kill. Hence this warning, a warning especially vivid to us on the *Paradise,* wielders of stolen fire."

"Your interpretation, Sayati Elk, hardly seems the simplest and most legitimate; it's infinitely complicated."

"It's the simplest explanation that accounts for the arrogantly directed history of our island, Ingram, and by 'arrogantly directed' I don't mean to imply that we—Atarite and Mansuecerian alike—don't share in the shame of our failures and the simple pride of our glories, only that we have been measured against an alien standard and made to suffer unduly for the squalid aspects of our nature—even though They have altered that!" He delivered this little oration heatedly, as if it had been rehearsed a thousand times but never before spoken.

I said, "Aren't you seeking a scapegoat, Sayati Elk, a scapegoat external to ourselves?"

"I absolve humanity of nothing! At the same time I refuse to designate humanity itself as a scapegoat, as the Parfects decided six or seven thousand years ago it must be so designated. That view is abhorrent to me, as abhorrent as the utter denial of our guilt. —I resent the suppression of humanity, I resent the Parfects' self-undertaken Sitting in Judgment."

"And if humankind destroys himself?"

"He must be free to do so, even if he does it over and over again until the last sterile coupling of the species. Or until he learns."

"And if he doesn't learn?"

"Then his viability as a creature worthy of the cornucopian gifts of chaos has proved altogether too weak and he must die—cursing himself, mind you, not that cruel but munificent chaos. His passing will have, must have, the grandeur of tragedy. That much is evident, Ingram, that much is clear."

I looked away from his intent, naked face. Ahead of us, off to the right, the hazy blue line of Ongladred's southern coast was becoming visible; we had successfully rounded the cape. The ships in harbor at Mershead and Brechtlin must have had to endure the shock waves of the pounding we ourselves had ridden out at sea. Now, however, the clear sky and the windless air mocked our memories; the planet basked.

"Could your sloak—whether native or quasi-organic—have caused an upheaval like the one we just survived, Sayati Elk? Legends have it that the thing's so thin its body has almost no width at all."

"The legends are legends, and even if true, the activation of the monster's biocybernetic consciousness from the Parfects' orbiter would generate enough energy both to thicken the sloak's immensely attenuated membrane and to stir up the sea in the process. Once drawn together for its assault on Ongladred, the sloak becomes as formidable a sea beast as any that has ever lived—either in Mansueceria's oceans or in Earth's."

"For everything, you have an answer." *Didn't Sayati Elk's resurrection of the dead for the purposes of his dramaturgy have a kind of parallel, a kind of affinity, with the Parfects' "activation" of the sloak (assuming of course, that the old man's hypothesis was correct)?* That was a question which I didn't ask, but which I decided to think about. There were a great many questions that I would have to think about in the days, the years, ahead.

"No, not answers, Ingram, *theories*—all of which I intensely believe in, since they are better than all others and since they are mine."

Gabriel Elk said this without a hint of haughtiness, but I wanted to deflate him somehow, wanted to disabuse him of his own intricate but annoyingly logical theory. I asked,

"What about the two-thousand-year cycle of the sloak? Isn't that too regular for an expedient that you claim is punitive? Does humankind reach the brink of forbidden knowledge with so inhuman a precision each two thousand years?"

"The sloak has come only twice before, even according to legend. How can we compute its cycle with any accuracy? Besides, Ingram, this—the Year of the Halcyon Panic—is not the only year that men have predicted the return of the sloak, the destruction of the species. Men are superstitious beings; they read numbers into everything. Eventually their mystical numbers become the basis of a numinous science. Oh, it's beautiful and frightening, this becoming, Ingram, one which always unworks itself only to evolve again. The cycle of the sloak? It is science and superstition compromising their separate integrities through the mediation of numbers."

"Dear Maz," I said. "Spare me more of this. Spare me."

Gabriel Elk threw his head back and laughed, laughed with hearty abandon, as if his breath would puff our sails in the breathless day and billow us jauntily into Brechtlin's harbor—a galleon of heroes ready for their gallons of haoma, a crew of gallant murderers hoping to inundate their crime in the masker panacea.

Amazingly enough, in two hours Captain Chant and our seamen, having wrung the air for its faintest stirring, took us into the recently wave-lashed but now silent harbor, and after fifteen days at sea we disembarked upon our native soil. Behind us, a sky full of masts and sails. Before us, the port, a road, and all of Ongladred.

In the flush of this excitement I forgot that it was I who had incinerated the enemy, nearly eight hundred human beings—until, as I left the *Paradise*, I saw Gentleman Gnot staring after me.

xviii

Gabriel Elk and I rented a wagon in Brechtlin, had the photon-director loaded into it, and drove not to Lunn but along the coastal road toward Mershead. "The weapon is mine," the old man told me. "I don't have to take it back to Chancellor Blaine; he'll discover soon enough, without our telling him, that the *Paradise* is in harbor." It was dark when we reached Stonelore. Oddly, I felt that I had come home too; that this arena of rock and sand and artificial light belonged more certainly to me than did any of the tract on which the Atarite Palace sits.

Bethel and Robin Coigns met us in front of Grotto House. That there were only the two of them was in itself an ominous thing.

Bethel kissed her husband. Then she stepped back from

him, her hands still on his shoulders, and said, "Gareth is dead, Gabriel." Then she ran her hand slowly over her husband's head, backward from the brow. "Someone has told you already?"

"No. You are the first." He pulled his wife to him, and they embraced—a silent, undemonstrative, somehow expressive embrace. Coigns and I stood apart, not so much excluded from this sharing as simply incapable of comprehending its intensity. Then Gabriel Elk drew his wife with him toward the house, the woman almost an extension of himself, he almost an extension of her, the two of them incomprehensibly and reproachfully whole. "Ingram," he said, "Robin, come with us." We followed. Silently.

Later, in the arras-hung dining chamber, we talked—while the beardless Gareth's almost tangible presence hovered in our words and breaths. The stone table was between us like a funeral slab; the Atarite Palace and the provinces of Ongladred were reduced in our minds to ghostly greys on a battle chart. Before a single dead loved one, the concepts of civilization defended and honor reaffirmed dissolve into fume and blow away, like cannon smoke. Even with no one of my own to mourn, I knew that much; the knowledge had grown in me.

"He was killed four days ago," Robin Coigns was telling us. "Those machines that Sayati Snow and Master Gordon brought up to below Firthshir had turned it all around, the fighting, you know, and the Pelagans had started back up north, all the way through Vestacs and Eenlich, too, it looked like. The boy he was killed in the per-suit Field-Pavan Barrow ordered right after the machines turned 'em around. Then, when he sees they can still kill us, you know, while we're per-suing 'em, ole Barrow calls it all off and we just let 'em go, just let 'em run—but Gareth he was already dead, Sayati Elk, he was already lost, along with a mess of others, all of 'em on-the-line fellows, too."

There was silence.

Bethel Elk sat with her hands folded in her lap, as regal in her silken green gown as I had ever seen Our Shathra Anna. Gabriel kept his gaze down, apparently directing it at his heavy, rope-veined hands.

Then he said: "An irony, Robin. An almost maudlinly predictable one. Irony, a part of my trade; a philosophical joke to work on my creations. Now it comes home to haunt me."

Bethel said, "Forget that, Gabriel. We will mourn awhile."

The old man looked up; he looked at Robin Coigns. "Where is Gareth? Was he buried in the north?"

"He's under," Robin said simply. "He's in the tunnel 'twixt Grotto House and Stonelore."

"Here?"

"Aye, Sayati Elk."

"How?"

"He took a rifle ball in the throat, sir, through the Adam's apple so his wind was cut; the ball lodged there, you see. It wasn't meant for me to be beside him then, I guess. Others came running for me and took me back, but by then our officers knew him for your son and called for haomycin to go into his blood so as to get him back here 'fore he stiffened. I was shunted off to one hand, Sayati Elk, and most near cried, and watched 'em do what they had to. Gareth he lay in the midst of all this scrambling, you know, and bled the life all out and couldn't see me no more than if he was blind, his eyes gone back and his face just as still as old milk. He got home 'fore I did, Sayati Elk—*preserved*, sort of. They took him off that way, with nothing for me to do but watch. I near cried, sir."

"We put Gareth in a preservator, Gabriel," Bethel said.

"Which one? They were all full."

"They're empty now, Gabriel. Except for Gareth's, and Bronwen Lief's. After you left, I had some men come out from Lunn and give the other dead ones their second funerals. They were burned, our actors, all of them together—in the place we always burn them—at the end of the summer. I couldn't leave them sleeping in that heartless ice, Gabriel."

"Why did you spare the girl?"

"I don't know. Because she was new—newer than the others. Because I had seen her dance."

"I want to see Gareth," the old man said.

I asked, "May I go with you?"

After an almost imperceptible pause the old man said, "Please, Ingram."

We excused ourselves. Bethel and Coigns permitted us to go without them. They had seen the boy, and they knew Gabriel's wish for what it was, a plea for one last, unhampered moment of communion. Perhaps I was less sensitive than they, for I knew this, too, and should not have gone with him—but I felt that he would have refused to let me go if my presence had threatened to throw up a wall between him and his dead son. I had to go with him. Down into the programming room, into the dark tunnel, into the dormitory room for corpses. Sensing my need to accompany him, Elk had said yes.

And so we left the dining chamber, walked down the hallway of luminous panels, and rode the elevator into the very womb and bowels of Grotto House. My sensation of going home grew more pronounced, more and more uncanny.

Then we were in the icy preservator room, among the ranked coffins and the upended storage tanks of lox. A faint musical seething played in my ears. Our breaths took shape in the air like dreamlike sails; we had voyaged into a numinous place, a world whose deities were enshrined in ice and plastic. Four of the shrines were empty, but in the two closest to the door we found the daughter of Josu and Rhia Lief and the newly slain son of Gabriel and Bethel Elk. These young people were the numens of the preservator room, guardian spirits whose frozen youth mocked their guardianship. Were they not too primevally vernal for such a custodial godhood? I stared through crystal at first the woman, then the young man—whose throat was swaddled in a wide bandage.

Bronwen Lief looked different to me. Her face was not a whit altered from the first time I had seen her, long ages ago, back before the spring had come. But the smirk I had then read in the twist of her mouth seemed not at all sinister now; it was not even a smirk, it was instead a wholly natural flaw, human and therefore reassuring.

As for Gareth, he looked no different, no different at all—except that his sparse, adolescent beard had matured into stubble. If Bethel had had him shaved before committing him to the preservator, then even in death his facial hair had continued to grow. So: His corpse's features were fresh and youthful, but touched with the beginnings of a revivifying weariness.

Wearing frost-gloves, Gabriel adjusted the cryostat on Bronwen Lief's preservator. With the cryostat he could take the temperature within each coffin up and down a limited scale of cold in a very brief time, although the preservator room itself remained at a constant 0° C. in case of separate cryostat malfunctions. As the temperature in Bronwen's unit rose toward that of the room itself, the old man leaned over his dead son and studied the boy's face. "He was growing into himself, Ingram. He was just on the verge of growing into the wholeness of himself."

My hands, for warmth, were in my armpits. I was behind the old man, and as he leaned over the preservator I noticed for the first time an angry red gleam on the back of his head, his mottled, naked skull. It was a nevus, a birthmark, a magenta discoloration just to the right of and a little above the brain stem. Before I could stop myself I had reached out and touched the tiny mark.

Gabriel Elk turned slowly and looked at me. I withdrew my hand, the image of the nevus clearly before me even though the old man had turned. "You have a mark back there," I said.

Briefly his face was inscrutable. Then he smiled and his eyes crinkled into almost Mongoloid slits: a pleasant, joy-etched smile. "Ingram, I'd almost forgotten the mark. When I was little my father used to brush my hair aside there and tell me that I'd been branded by the Evil One, by Ahriman himself."

"Yes," I said. "It's like a scorpion, a little scorpion with its stinger raised."

"My father always told me of the blemish with a smile, as if joking, but he upset me more than he knew, and for a time I dreaded his touch—his reminder to me of something I knew was back there but couldn't actually see for myself. My father was a Mansuecerian, Ingram, a masker, and I knew that I was somehow different from him. For a long time I believed the difference lay in the scorpion mark, that it and only it was what set me apart from my family and everyone else."

"That mark probably made your father uneasy, Sayati Elk. It's frighteningly perfect, it might almost be a tattoo."

"He told me that, too, Ingram—though not in those words. And when I reached adolescence I ceased resenting his uneasy banter about the birthmark; I understood his uneasiness, his ill-expressed love. I understood what I was and how the differences in what we were didn't finally matter. But I kept waiting for him to express—in some uncharacteristically flamboyant way—the love he didn't know how to articulate."

Gabriel Elk rubbed the spot I had touched. "Oh, those are

mostly good memories, Ingram, almost from another life, they're so far away." He rubbed the spot and smiled.

Then he abruptly turned and began disconnecting some of the apparatus affixed to Bronwen Lief's preservator. Apparently he was not going to let those memories overwhelm him. As we had done several times during the summer, he pulled the coffin on its coasterlike wheels out of its moorings and pushed it toward the door. He gave me a pair of frost-gloves.

"What are you doing?" I asked.

"Going back to work. Will you help me?" He returned to the young woman's preservator after giving me the gloves and began to roll it toward me. I opened the door for him, and together we pushed the gleaming white fuselage through the tunnel and into the programming room. I couldn't believe that it was beginning again, I didn't know how to react.

Once inside the programming room, however, the old man said, "Go upstairs and go to bed. Take Gareth's room. I want you to have it."

I hesitated. "Sayati Elk, I can't tell Mistress Elk I'm taking her son's room. Not now."

"Tell her. She'll understand."

"Are you going to stay here?"

"For a while. Go on. Go upstairs. Go to bed."

Reluctantly I rode the elevator up. Alone in the main hallway, I felt like a figure in a photographic negative, like the light-blackened obverse of myself. Then, in her silken green gown, Bethel Elk came toward me out of the glare of the corridor's wall panels and restored color to the microcosmic world of Grotto House.

I told her what her husband had told me to tell her. She put her hand on my arm. She led me to Gareth's room. The door opened for me. She said, "Go in, Ingram, and sleep well." The door closed behind me. And momentarily I felt again like a black figure on a white ground—until I brushed against a wall panel and a flood of yellow light reversed things once more.

The room was exactly like the one I had slept in before Gareth's death—except that at various places about the room Gareth had put on display pieces of his idiosyncratic statuary. Sinuous trees carved out of stone, every piece a gnarled and leafless tree. I picked up the sculpture next to my bed. It was unfinished, almost as if the boy had realized that no matter how expert his hands became or how exemplary his vision, in execution his trees would inevitably be dead and petrified before he could complete them; as if he had realized this and given up the attempt as foolish.

The tree I was holding may have been the last one he ever worked on. I set it down and stretched out on the dead boy's bed.

xix

The next day Arngrim Blaine appeared at Stonelore. His arrival coincided with Robin Coigns' departure for Brechtlin in the wagon we had rented the previous afternoon; the ostler was going to return the wagon and ride back to us on the horse following the wagon on a short tether.

As Coigns left the upland arena and joggled on the wagon seat down the dusty hillside, we saw the Chancellor's equipage approaching from Lunn. In a red billow, wagon and carriage passed each other. Only two Atarite guardsmen rode beside the Chancellor, and they did not venture into the arena with his sleek, ebony coach; instead, they halted and took up positions outside the rock wall, as had the charioteers on that night when Bronwen Lief danced and the reivers drew down on us from their blind. Had we learned nothing?

147

But the war was over, I reminded myself, we had successfully beat back the bringers of ruin. I had murdered a few
myself.

"Welcome," Sayati Elk said when Chancellor Blaine
stepped down from his coach. "Once again, we're honored."

The man with the roan tooth tilted his head and clasped
the old man's hands in his own. "It's I who should extend the
welcome, Sayati Elk. Welcome home to Ongladred. Your
countrymen and your countrymen's rulers have proved to be
more flexible than many"—the Chancellor gave me a significant look—"felt to be possible. Our Shathra Anna has
fathomless reservoirs of flexibility; she ordered me to pay
you a visit when it became apparent that you weren't going
to come into Lunn of your own volition."

"An inconvenience to you," Gabriel Elk said, "for which
I apologize."

The three of us were crossing the arena, walking slowly. I
said, "Why exactly did she send you out here, Chancellor
Blaine?"

He didn't answer at once. But finally he did say, "To offer
both congratulations and condolences, Sayati Elk. And these
tasks I undertake willingly. Don't speak of inconvenience.
There is none, none whatever. I'm only sorry that your son's
death diminishes the joy you must feel in your homecoming."

Elk said nothing. He opened the wrought-iron gate across
the foyer to Grotto House and led us inside. Bethel joined
us, and since the day was fair and unseasonably warm, we
went through the foyer to the house's open, central courtyard. All of us but the old man took up seats on the stone
benches there. Elk, his bald head absorbing rather than reflecting the sunlight, stood with his back to us. I could not
help looking at the scorpion mark above his runneled nape.
It focused my attention.

I heard him saying, "Robin tells me that Sayati Snow and

Master Gordon swept the enemy before them with the ease of minor deities. And that we pursued our retreating enemy."

Blaine responded, "And Captain Chant tells me that Master Marley destroyed six Pelagan warships as if they were soap bubbles waiting for the lance."

"Five," I said.

"Was that pursuit necessary?" Bethel asked, picking up a dropped thread.

"That's a determination only Field-Pavan Barrow could make, Mistress Elk. I am no tactician."

"Where are the photon-directors that Snow and Gordon used?" Gabriel Elk asked. "They must be returned to me, Chancellor, that was a principal stipulation of our agreement."

"In safekeeping at the Atarite Palace, Sayati Elk. Where is the one you and Master Marley used aboard the *Paradise*?"

"Beneath Grotto House. Coigns carried it down for me last night, and I removed its chemical power source." Elk turned and faced us. The leaves of the blood lily behind him caught the sunlight and showed us their velvet, crimson underbellies. "It's a disemboweled machine, Chancellor. Dead."

"Well, while it lived, it reveled. So be it."

This remark seemed to me inordinately tactless. I stood up. I walked off a few paces down one of the stone paths in the courtyard. Then I halted, still within speaking distance of the others. Around me: blood lilies, autumn azaleas, the hard yellow berries of the ahura-wood, the inner walls of Grotto House. Gabriel, Bethel, and the Chancellor formed the points of a triangle which excluded me—until I realized that I had simply extended the geometry of our disenchantment. I was a fourth point, I meant too.

"You've offered congratulations and condolences," Sayati Elk said. "Surely that doesn't comprise the whole purpose of your journey?"

"Actually it does. The only other thing Our Shathra asked me to do was to bring Ingram back to Lunn with me. He's handled his responsibilities capably, and we desire to reward him."

"Then let me stay here," I said.

Arngrim Blaine looked at me as one looks at a presumptuous child; but for the carnelian flash of his tooth, his smile would have been fatherly. "A decision such as that is out of my hands, Ingram. Nor could Our Shathra Anna make it without knowing Sayati and Mistress Elk's feelings."

"Does Our Shathra Anna seek to reward me, too?" Gabriel asked.

"Certainly." The Chancellor's eyes blinked rapidly.

"Then I ask as my reward that which Ongladred owes me. A son. If Ingram Marley wishes to stay here at Grotto House, we wish him to stay as our son."

Bethel said, "Grant Ingram his request, Chancellor Blaine, and you have granted ours as well."

"Ingram is rather old to be acquiring parents, Mistress Elk."

"Oh, indeed yes," she said.

"Besides, it's not only for his personal qualities that I wish him to stay here," the old man added. "A fortnight from now I intend to present a neuro-masque in the Stonelore amphitheatre, and Master Marley will be of invaluable assistance to me in the comptroller room. Tell Our Shathra Anna that she is invited, that the masque will commemorate her reign in dance and song."

And so it happened, in that exchange of words, that I gave up my place in the Atarite Court, my status as a dirt-runner, my incompetently executed duties as a member of the Eyes and Ears of Our Shathra Anna. As the Chancellor and Sayati Elk and Mistress Elk talked, my past fell away.

I looked up at Maz. I was conscious of the fluttering colors of the courtyard, leaves peripherally afire with burnt red and smoky emerald, and of the wan circle of the sun shedding its summer scales down the sky. My past had fallen away, even that part of it including my sojourn with the Elks. It had not disappeared; it lay at my feet like dead leaves or shed scales, and I had the power either to collapse into it or to stride out of its alluring, brittle debris. I was still held, but the coils were off, the colors were golden.

The conversation of the others went on around me as I tried to read the future in Maz' outlines, to adjust to the new skin that I still had no right to. The morning passed, the afternoon passed, and somewhere in this evanescent progression Arngrim Blaine found a moment in which to bid us goodbye and depart.

Before I could think what had happened to me, to all of us, I was in Gareth's bed once more, hypnotized by the tangled shadow cast upon the wall by one of the young Elk's meticulously carven stone trees. I could not sleep. My mind was in the branches of the shadow. I lay tangled in the flown, leafless day. Too many things had happened, but the only one who seemed aware of their significance was I. Then, faint footfalls began to resonate in the shadow's branches. It was an illusion. The footfalls were coming from the hallway, from the corridor outside my door. I lay listening to them even after they had gone. A long time later I got up and left Gareth's room. Down the illuminated corridor I walked, placing my feet in the shadows of the footfalls that had preceded me.

I was in front of the elevator. I rode the elevator down.

In the programming room I found Gabriel Elk bent over the corpse of his son, working with liver-spotted and untrembling hands to turn the boy into an actor. As he worked, he talked. He talked in a low, almost emotionless monotone whose very lack of coherence was poignant.

Beside the table on which Gareth lay was the preservator I had seen him in the night before. It stood open and empty, like the casing of one of those fabled bombs that had so long ago virtually destroyed our spawning place, making our planet the home of a preemptive neo-human species that had exiled us, masker and Atarite, to the darkling islands of a northern sea on a world eight hundred light-years from Earth. The whirring of a small computer and the tiny hands sweeping across each tube in an array of cathode-ray tubes (these last on the face of a toposcopic unit opposite the table itself) made the room an eerie place. Gabriel Elk's voice droned on above the sound of the computer; his hands continued to wire, and probe, and snip, and hover, lingering now clinically, now out of something profoundly unscientific.

Before the old man could see me, I turned and left the programming room. Upstairs, the boy's inert trees were waiting for me, frozen in time, tangled in my own nascent memory.

xx

I have been at Stonelore almost two years. The sloak has not returned to Ongladred, and the bonfires on the beaches have long since been allowed to go out. Perhaps there is not any such creature; perhaps the Parfects—in their infinite, condescending wisdom—have granted us their penultimate reprieve. I don't care anymore, I live as if my fate were in no one's hands but my own. When I look at the night sky, I see only the Shattered Moons, nothing sinister, nothing quietly malign—and I hold my breath and genuflect before their random, concerted beauty.

The photon-directors that Sayati Snow and Master Gordon used against the Pelagans have still not been returned to us. Our Shathra Anna and Chancellor Blaine have each been to Stonelore twice since the morning I was granted my freedom from the Atarite Court, and they now assure us that the weapons were dismantled in Lunn.

I don't know how we should accept this news. Gabriel Elk doesn't believe it, he thinks Blaine is lying.

As for our enemies, they have ceased to attack our goods and people even in the small reiving parties for which they have always been famous. For what purpose, then, can our rulers want a weapon like the photon-director?

We know. We are not naive.

But uncertainty about the final handling of the ones wielded by Sayati Snow and Master Gordon still plagues us. It is impossible to demand of Our Shathra Anna any sort of clarification.

Gabriel Elk, however, has clarified a point that used to deprive me of sleep. Why a place like Stonelore? Why the agony and the frustration to which he yearly subjects himself?

"Because one day I am going to make them weep, Ingram, one day I am going to make them weep." Until that day, despite the old man's and Bethel's undoubtedly justified reproaches, they will continue to be maskers to me. Not Mansuecerians; maskers. But they will weep, that day will come—I'm certain of it. And when it comes the citizens of this island nation will cremate the dead when they die, and I, since I have no talent for dramaturgy or sculpture, may become the first living actor in all our history.

Nevertheless, the day is coming when they will weep.